THE LIGHTS GO ON AGAIN

Born in Edmonton, Alberta, Kit Pearson graduated in English at the University of Alberta before going on to get her MLS at the University of British Columbia and an MA in children's literature at the Center for the Study of Children's Literature, Simmons College, Boston.

A former librarian as well as a writer, Ms Pearson has written several novels, including *The Daring Game*, *A Handful of Time* and a trilogy consisting of *The Sky Is Falling*, *Looking at the Moon* and *The Lights Go On Again*. Her most recent novel, *Awake and Dreaming*, won the Governor General's Award for Children's Literature.

Christmas 1998

from: Grandma & Grandpa

He who would valiant be
'Gainst all disaster

John Bunyan and others

THE LIGHTS GO ON AGAIN

Kit Pearson

Puffin Books

PUFFIN BOOKS
Published by the Penguin Group
Penguin Books Canada Ltd, 10 Alcorn Avenue, Toronto, Ontario, Canada M4V 3B2
Penguin Books Ltd, 27 Wrights Lane, London W8 5TZ, England
Penguin Putnam Inc., 375 Hudson Street, New York, New York 10014, U.S.A.
Penguin Books Australia Ltd, Ringwood, Victoria, Australia
Penguin Books (NZ) Ltd, cnr Rosedale and Airborne Roads, Albany, Auckland 1310,
New Zealand

Penguin Books Ltd, Registered Offices: Harmondsworth, Middlesex, England

First published in Viking by Penguin Books Canada Limited, 1993
Published in Puffin Books, 1994

7 9 10 8 6

Publisher's note: This book is a work of fiction. Names, characters, places and incidents either are the product of the author's imagination or are used fictitiously, and any resemblance to actual persons living or dead, events, or locales is entirely coincidental.

Manufactured in Canada

Canadian Cataloguing in Publication Data
Pearson, Kit, 1947-
The lights go on again

ISBN 0-14-036412-9

I. Title

PS8581.E37W53 1994   jC813'.54   C93-093820-8
PZ7.P43Wh 1994

Visit Penguin Canada's web site at **www.penguin.ca**

For Ian

Contents

I

What Am I Going To Do?

The large boy hulked in front of Gavin on the sidewalk, blocking his way.

"Hold it right there, Stoakes."

Gavin looked behind him, to where he'd just left Tim and Roger at the corner. They were already too far away to call back. And it was no use running. Mick could easily catch him.

"What do you want?" Gavin breathed.

Mick's mean face came closer. His eyes glittered like hard blue marbles. "I want you to do me a favour."

"Wh-what?"

"I need some cash. Bring me two bucks tomorrow morning. You can meet me at the school flagpole before the bell. Understand?"

"But I haven't *got* two dollars!"

"Then get it. I know your ma's rich."

"She isn't really my mother," said Gavin. "She's not even related to me. She's just looking after me and my sister until the war is over. My real mother lives in England."

Mick grabbed Gavin's arm and gave it a savage twist. "So what? You live with her in that fancy house, doncha? Bring me the money by tomorrow morning — or you'll be jelly!"

Gavin tried to curb his tears. Pain blazed up his arm. "Okay, Mick. Could you please let go? You're hurting me!"

Mick gave one more tortuous twist, then freed Gavin's arm. Gavin picked up his speller out of the snow and fled, the bigger boy's words shouting behind him, "Don't forget — tomorrow morning before the bell!"

The icy December air made his lungs ache, but Gavin didn't stop running until he reached the towering house at the end of one of the winding streets. He pounded up its wide steps and slammed the door behind him. Safe!

"Is that you, Gavin?" Hanny, the cook, came out of the kitchen, wiping floury hands on her apron. "Why are you so out of breath?" She pulled off his tuque. "And look at your hair — you're sweating!"

"I — just — felt — like — running," panted Gavin. "Where's Bosley?" Usually his springer spaniel waited for him at the end of the block.

"Norah took him for a walk. She got out of school early today. And your aunts are having tea at Mrs Bond's. Would you like something to eat?"

"Yes, please. Can I have it in my room?"

Hanny gave him a glass of milk and an apple. Gavin carried them carefully up the stairs. He changed out of his school breeks, rubbing the itchy places behind his knees where the wool chafed. He sat down on the rug beside his bed and tried to eat.

But his tears escaped. They burned against his cold cheeks, as his chest still heaved.

"Stop it!" he whispered fiercely. "*Crybaby . . .*" Gavin sniffed deeply, wiped his eyes on the bedspread and began to nibble the apple. *Think . . .*

Two dollars! He'd never be able to find that much money by tomorrow. He glanced at the iron bank shaped like a bear on his desk, but he knew it only contained the fifteen cents he was saving to go to the movies on Saturday.

Tomorrow was the day Aunt Florence gave him a quarter to take to school for his weekly war savings stamp. If he kept that and the fifteen cents and next week's stamp money and allowance quarter . . .

He counted on his fingers. That made only ninety cents. Besides, it was stealing. And he knew Mick wouldn't wait.

He couldn't ask Aunt Florence for two whole dollars without telling her why he needed it. And he knew enough not to tattle on Mick. Ken Cunningham had last month. Mick got the strap and Ken appeared in school the next week with a black eye. He told everyone he'd fallen playing hockey.

Gavin winced as he lifted his glass to drain it. His arm still smarted. Why was the meanest boy in the school suddenly picking on *him*?

Ever since Mick Turner had arrived in September he had been the terror of Prince Edward School. He was large for grade seven — even the grade eights were afraid of him. He bullied alone, stalking the corridors, the washrooms and the playground for his victims. So far Gavin and his friends had managed to avoid him — until today.

Gavin found *The Boy's King Arthur* on his shelf, climbed onto the bed and opened the book to the picture of Sir Launcelot facing Sir Turquine.

"I am Sir Launcelot, the bravest knight in the world," he whispered. Then he read what Sir Launcelot had done to Sir Turquine, how he "leaped upon him fiercely as a lion, and got him by the banner of his helmet, and so he plucked him down on his knees, and anon he rased his helm, and then he smote his neck asunder." For a second or two Gavin felt as satisfied as if he had cut off Mick's head. Then he clapped the book shut.

In real life he wouldn't even attack Mick with his fists. It wasn't just that Mick was so much bigger. It was because Gavin hated fighting. Lots of the other grade five boys got into fights. But it made Gavin feel sick to think of hitting someone, or being hit back. He was such a coward! Sir Launcelot wasn't afraid of fighting. Or of bullies like Mick.

But fighting was dangerous. Once a long time ago, when Gavin had been five, *everything* had been dangerous. Then there was talk of Hitler invading England, and bombs, and enemy planes crashing. But after he and his older sister Norah had come to Canada as "war guests" he'd been safe.

Lately, though, even his security in Toronto had begun to crumble. The war, which had been going on as long as Gavin could remember, was ending. The grown-ups talked about how the Germans were being driven farther and farther back. Troops had landed in France on D-Day and now Paris was liberated. In school they sang songs about the end of the war: "It's a Lovely Day Tomorrow," "The White Cliffs of Dover" and "When the Lights Go On Again."

Of course Gavin wanted the Allies to beat Germany and Italy and Japan. But once the war was over, there would be no reason for him and Norah to stay in Canada. They'd have to go back to England, to that place where he had felt so *unsafe*. To a scary new country and a scary new school. To a family he barely remembered, though Norah talked about them all the time.

Gavin shivered and, as usual, tried not to think about it. But it was so hard not to, when his parents' letters talked about their return, when Aunt Florence and Aunt Mary kept giving him sad looks and when Norah, especially, was so excited about going back.

"Just wait, Gavin," she said. "You'll really like our village. There's a pond where you can fish and woods to play in."

I like it *here,* Gavin wanted to answer — but that would show what a scaredy-cat he was.

He tried to think of how brave all the men were who were fighting in the war. Like Andrew, Aunt Florence's great-nephew — he was a soldier

stationed in Italy. Gavin and Tim and Roger often
pretended they were fighting in the war, but Gavin
knew he'd never have the guts to really do it. Just as
he didn't have the guts to fight Mick.

Gavin flipped up his eiderdown on each side,
forming a snug cocoon around him. He tried not to
cry again. If only Bosley were here to comfort him.
Or *Creature* . . .

Creature was the name of his small stuffed elephant. When Gavin was little he took him every-
where and talked to him as if he were real. He'd
never do that now, of course — not now that he was
ten. But he wished he still had him.

A year ago he'd lost Creature. The family had
helped him search the whole house. "He must have
fallen out of your pocket outside," said Aunt
Florence. "Would you like me to buy you a new
elephant?"

"No, thank you." Gavin had smiled and pretended he didn't care . . .

He sat up and wiped his eyes. *Think!* Think
about *Mick,* not about a stupid toy elephant! He had
only this evening to find the money.

"Norah . . . can I talk to you?" Gavin stood in
Norah's doorway after dinner.

"Sure! I need a break anyway." Norah turned
around from her desk and stretched as Gavin came
into her room. It was in the tower, the highest part
of the house. Whenever he was up here he felt safe;
like being in a fortress.

Should he tell her about Mick? He studied his

sister. Now that Norah had started high school she had turned into a "bobby-soxer." She and her best friend, Paige Worsley, looked like twins, in their Sloppy Joe sweaters, saddle shoes and pleated skirts. Norah wore lipstick whenever she was out of the house. Photographs of Frank Sinatra plastered her walls. Last month, when Aunt Florence had been away in Montreal, Aunt Mary had let her have a slumber party. The house had resounded with the shrieks of six teen-age girls, as they played records, curled each other's long hair and talked on the telephone all evening. Aunt Mary, Hanny and Gavin had retreated to the kitchen to escape the racket.

But underneath her teen-age disguise Norah was still Norah: his kind older sister and his best friend. She was also the bravest person he knew.

That was why he couldn't tell her about Mick. She'd be so furious that someone was picking on her brother that she'd tell on Mick. Then he would be even meaner to Gavin.

"Well?" smiled Norah. "Why are you staring at me like that? What did you want to talk about?"

"Do you have any money?" Gavin asked quickly. "I need two dollars really fast."

"Two dollars!" Norah looked apologetic. "I'm sorry, Gavin, I'm broke. Why do you need so much?"

"I can't tell you."

"Oh. Well, why don't you ask Aunt Florence?"

"I can't tell her either," said Gavin, "and you know she wouldn't give it to me unless she knew why." He shrugged, as if it wasn't important. "It doesn't matter."

Aunt Mary's voice called up the stairs. "Ga-vin ... it's almost time for your programme."

"Coming down to listen to 'The Lone Ranger'?" Gavin asked her.

"Not tonight — I have to study! Maths is the first exam and I'm not nearly ready."

"I thought maths was your best subject." It was Gavin's worst.

Norah looked sheepish. "It usually is. But I missed some important parts of algebra when I was — um — out of school."

In October Norah had been suspended from high school for two days. She'd written an essay about how she didn't believe in war and how killing people was always wrong. When her teacher had given her a low mark she'd protested to the principal.

Gavin remembered how steadfast she'd been all through the huge fuss both at school and at home. The adults had called her "disrespectful," both to them and to her country, but not once had Norah faltered in her firm beliefs. No one, not even Aunt Florence, had been able to squash her. Finally her mark had been reluctantly raised and she'd returned to school in triumph.

Gavin sighed; if only *he* were unsquashable. "You'll do okay, Norah," he told her. "You always do."

"Thanks, Gavin." Her clear grey-green eyes searched his face. "Are you *sure* you don't want to tell me why you need so much money? Are you in some kind of trouble?"

Gavin almost told her. But he thought of Norah confronting *his* principal the way she had hers, and of Mick's reaction.

"I'm sure," he mumbled, turning to go.

Norah swivelled her chair back to her desk. "All right, then. I'd better get on with maths. I'm not looking forward to tomorrow morning!"

Neither am I! thought Gavin as he trudged down the two flights of stairs to the den.

Gavin tried to forget about Mick as the galloping music and the Lone Ranger's call of "Hi-yo, Silver ... away!" began his favourite Monday evening radio programme. He held open his speller as he listened but he couldn't concentrate on the list of words he was supposed to learn for tomorrow. Instead he let his mind fill with images of cowboys who always beat their enemies.

Aunt Florence and Aunt Mary knitted as they listened — long grey scarves for soldiers. Gavin put down his book and ran his fingers through Bosley's silky fur. The dog's loose skin was dark under his black patches and pale under his white ones. His long ears were the softest part of him; Gavin massaged one between his palms and Bosley thumped his tail in ecstasy.

When the programme was over, Gavin lay down on the floor and rested his head on the soothing warmth of Bosley's side. I wish I was a dog, he thought, as the problem of Mick came rushing back. Dogs never had to worry about anything.

"Turn to the news, Mary," Aunt Florence told her daughter. As usual, Gavin didn't listen. For most of his life he had sat with grown-ups around a radio while an announcer droned on about the war.

He watched his two guardians. Quiet, plump Aunt Mary, her greying hair in a neat bun, had a peaceful expression on her plain face. When her mother wasn't around she let him and Norah do whatever they liked, as if all three of them were Aunt Florence's children. She was always ready to listen or to laugh at a joke. *Safe . . .*

Aunt Florence was even safer. Gavin remembered the only other time in his life he had felt this scared: travelling on a big ship to Canada, then living in a hostel with lots of other children while they waited to be assigned to a home. During those endless, confusing days he had clung to one person after another for protection, but they had all been temporary. He'd had to leave the nice women on the boat and at the hostel who'd taken care of him. And Norah had been so wrapped up in her own misery, she hadn't noticed how much he needed her.

Then he had stepped into this solid house where majestic Aunt Florence had welcomed him warmly and claimed him as her own.

"Why do you like her so much?" Norah sometimes asked Gavin. She preferred Aunt Mary. Although she and Aunt Florence secretly respected each other, they had always had a stormy relationship.

Gavin couldn't explain. The older he got the

more he realized how conceited and snobby his guardian was. She was often unfair to both her daughter and Norah, and she drove Hanny wild with her bossiness. But whenever Norah and Hanny sat in the kitchen making fun of Aunt Florence, Gavin defended her. Her utter, rock-like confidence — and knowing that he was the most important person in the world to her — protected him.

"You let her baby you too much," was another thing Norah told him. "You should stand up to her more."

But he didn't mind all the hugs and kisses and mushy nicknames. Aunt Florence often told Gavin how much he was like Hugh, her son who had been killed long ago in another world war. Sometimes she went on too much about his clothes, or how blue his eyes were. But when he politely objected she would laugh, hug him, and stop.

Aunt Florence thought he was perfect — coward or not.

"You're growing so fast, sweetness," she smiled when the news was over. "That shirt is much too short in the sleeves. We'll have to get you some new clothes, so your parents don't think I haven't been taking good care of you."

She almost grimaced when she mentioned his parents. But quite often lately Aunt Florence had brought up the subject of Gavin and Norah's return to England, even though it was obviously painful to her. Gavin had overheard the social worker from the Children's Aid Society who had visited last month warn the aunts that they had to prepare them.

He turned over and buried his face in Bosley's neck, sniffing in his warm, musty smell. He couldn't imagine his life without these two women. It was even harder to think of leaving Bosley. He'd known, ever since Aunt Florence's brother Reg had "lent" him the dog the summer before last, that he'd have to give him back one day. He knew in his head that Bosley wasn't really his. But in his heart he was.

Moping over leaving Canada wasn't any help. The end of the war might be soon — but facing Mick was tomorrow!

"I've been thinking, Gavin," said Aunt Florence. "Now that you're ten, I don't see why you can't stay up until nine. Would you like that?"

"Oh, yes, *please*!" Gavin sat up with surprise, and both the aunts laughed. The more Aunt Florence made herself talk about the coming separation, the more she filled Gavin's life with treats to cushion the pain.

Gavin knew he was spoilt; his friends often told him so enviously. He probably *could* ask for two dollars and get it; but only for a good reason. If he could think up a convincing lie, Aunt Florence would believe it. She trusted him. She thought that he was worth trusting; that he was good. And he liked being good — like Sir Launcelot, and the Lone Ranger, and the Shadow, and the pilgrim they talked about in Sunday School.

If only he could be brave, as well.

It was swell to be able to stay up later. But Gavin's stomach lurched as he thought of the bully's words: " . . . or you'll be jelly." Which part of him would Mick hit first?

"Oh, Bosley," Gavin whispered, "What am I going to do?" He almost started crying again.

Aunt Mary got up and peeked out the window. "It's snowing again! You'll have good tobogganing tomorrow, Gavin."

Gavin didn't answer. All at once he had thought of a solution — for the time being, anyway.

He would pretend to be sick. Aunt Florence would let him stay home from school if he said he didn't feel well. That wasn't really a lie . . . he *didn't* feel well, not when he thought about being pounded by Mick.

Gavin opened his speller again, limp with relief. It was a coward's way out, but it was all he could think of.

II

The Big Snow

That night Gavin dreamt he was Superman. He picked up Mick by the scruff of his neck, flew to the top of a high building, whirled the bully around his head three times, and dropped him. Mick screamed all the way down until he landed with a *SPLAT* — just like in the comics.

Gavin woke up tangled in his sheet. His clock said six-thirty but he hadn't heard the milkman's horse clomping in his dreams the way he usually did. His windowpane rattled and a branch scraped against it.

He hopped out of bed and opened the curtains. Snow raged against the glass, as if trying to get in. A blizzard!

Gavin grinned — then frowned, as he remembered his plan. If he pretended to be sick, he couldn't enjoy the fresh snow. But he could go out *now*, then get back into bed before anyone was up.

"Come on, Boz!" Bosley looked up from his basket with sleepy surprise. He stretched his long front legs out of it, leaving his hindquarters in place as he decided whether or not to wake up. He lumbered to his feet, then stretched again with a complaining groan.

"Lazybones," chuckled Gavin, flinging on his clothes. "Get up. We're going *out*. For a *walk!*"

At the word "walk" Bosley jolted awake. He danced and whined around Gavin, his stubby black tail wagging furiously.

"Shh!" Gavin held the dog by the collar as they crept downstairs. In the hall he put on his jacket, ski pants, tuque, mitts and galoshes. Then he unlocked the front door and pushed at it. It wouldn't budge.

"That's funny." He went into the kitchen and unlocked that door. But it, too, was stuck. He peeked out of the window.

"Wow . . ." The snow came halfway up the panes and the back yard was a whirling landscape. Gavin pushed at the door again but the snow blocked it. Bosley scratched at it and whined.

"You need to go out, don't you boy? But we're trapped!"

Gavin thought a minute. Then he hauled the kitchen table over to the window, stood on it, pulled down the upper sash and pushed out the storm window. Snow and cold air rushed into the warm kitchen. He poked out his head and looked down. The drifts were so high it probably wouldn't hurt to simply fall into them.

"Come on, Boz, you go first." Gavin lifted Bosley onto the slippery tabletop, climbed up himself and put the dog's front paws on top of the open window. His hind legs scrabbled for a foothold and he whined again, his liquid brown eyes looking back imploringly at Gavin.

"Be *brave*," Gavin told him. "Jump!" But Bosley kept whining and trying to get off the table. Gavin sighed. His dog was a coward too. "Come on . . . pretend you're Lassie." With great difficulty — Bosley was almost as big as he was — Gavin hoisted the protesting dog and spilled him out of the window. Then he tumbled out after him.

Down they both dropped, like stones into water, until the snow stopped their fall. They emerged caked in white, Bosley sneezing violently and Gavin laughing.

He brushed off his face, but the wind blew more snow into it. He struggled to the front of the house; it was like wading through waist-high mud. Then he stopped in awe.

Gavin had seen lots of snow since he'd lived in Canada, but never as much as this. He blinked through the swaying curtain of flakes. The street, sidewalks and front yards merged into one white expanse. Each house had several feet of snow heaped on its roof, with tall drifts blown against its doors and lower windows. Every car was buried. Snowflakes scraped against his jacket, melted on his eyelashes and tickled his nose.

Gavin stood spellbound in the dim morning light. He put out his tongue to catch the flakes, feeling like an Arctic explorer — Nansen, he decided — setting foot in an untouched land.

Bosley had followed gingerly in Gavin's path. Now he began to play, springing out of the snow like a jack-in-the-box. Gavin leapt and stumbled after him, throwing sprays of snow into the air. His laughter and Bosley's barking rang out in the silent street.

The snow was seeping into Gavin's cloth jacket and he began to shiver. He started towards the house, then stopped.

How was he going to get back in? The open window was too high to reach and both doors were blocked. And if he were trapped outside, that meant Norah and Aunt Florence and Aunt Mary were trapped inside!

What would Sir Launcelot do? Or Nansen? He floundered to the back yard and looked around. Then he spied the snow shovel under the porch, where Hanny's husband had left it the last time he'd shovelled the snow. He picked it up and began working on the four-foot drift blocking the back door.

His sore arm made it difficult to lift the shovel and he had to keep stopping to pound snow off the blade. Sweat ran down his forehead and his breath steamed around him. He pretended he was Nansen again and hummed to himself as he imagined freeing his fellow explorers from their igloo. The snow blew back almost as fast as he cleared it, but finally he had shovelled away enough to jerk open the door. He and Bosley ran through the kitchen into the hall.

"Wake up, everyone!" Gavin shouted. "I've rescued you!"

By breakfast the glow from the family's praise, which made Gavin feel like a hero, had worn off. While he was outside he had completely forgotten about Mick. He couldn't pretend to be sick now that he'd demonstrated so much healthy vigour.

"I've never *seen* so much snow!" marvelled Aunt Mary. "It must be a record!"

Aunt Florence brought in their breakfast. "I'm sure Hanny won't make it in at all today. And the milkman probably won't either, or the bread wagon. We're almost out of both. Only one piece of toast each, please."

Gavin looked out the window at the shifting white world. He glanced across the table at Norah, who smiled back. She was obviously hoping for the same thing he was. Then the radio confirmed it: all Toronto schools were closed.

"Hurray!" shouted Norah. "No exams!"

Gavin couldn't stop grinning as his fear rolled away. It would return tomorrow, but right now he had a whole day of freedom from Mick.

The holiday stretched to two days; two days when the city was paralysed by what everyone later called "the big snow." The grown-ups looked grave as calamities kept being reported on the radio. Several people died of over-exertion as they struggled through the drifts. A streetcar was overturned on Queen Street, trapping everyone inside. By Wednesday thirteen people had died and all deliveries were still delayed.

But for Gavin and his friends the blizzard was a profitable adventure. He and Norah strapped on their skis and struggled to the local store, where the owner allowed one quart of milk a customer. After the snow finally stopped falling, every young person in the neighbourhood began to shovel. They shovelled paths to doors. They shovelled sidewalks. They shovelled out cars. Gavin thought his arms would fall off, they ached so much. But it was worth it to feel like a hero again, as the people he shovelled out thanked him warmly. Best of all, many of them insisted on paying.

"You shouldn't take money," said Norah sternly, when he told her how old Mr Chapman had given him a quarter. "This is an emergency!"

"I tried to refuse but he said I had to!" said Gavin.

"Oh, all right. I guess it's okay as long as you don't ask."

By Wednesday afternoon Gavin had $3.15 — more money than he'd ever had in his life. Now he could face Mick when school opened again, and even have some left over.

"You'll always remember this, Norah and Gavin," said Aunt Mary that evening. "You can tell your grandchildren you experienced the worst storm Toronto has ever had."

They were relaxing in the den after dinner, as usual. The house had a huge living room but the family spent most of their time in the smaller, more comfortable den. Gavin sprawled on the floor, reading the funnies. Aunt Florence and Norah were huddled over a game of cribbage. Aunt Mary was unpacking Christmas tree ornaments, inspecting each one to see if it was broken.

"I think we should all be very proud of ourselves," said Aunt Florence. "Mary and I are pretty good cooks, aren't we? I believe my biscuits are even better than Hanny's. And you children were splendid, the way you got us milk and shovelled all that snow. I'm going to write to your parents and tell them."

They all beamed at each other, even Norah and Aunt Florence.

"I hear there's a shortage of Christmas trees and turkeys this year," said Aunt Mary.

"Then we'll do without a tree and have a goose instead of a turkey," said her mother calmly. "After all, we already do without using the car to have enough gas coupons for the summer." She put away the cards. "Beat you again, eh, Norah?" Norah grinned ruefully.

Aunt Florence took out *Oliver Twist* and began where she'd left off last time. This fall she had started reading aloud every evening, the way she did in the summers at Muskoka.

Gavin settled back against Bosley, who was snoozing peacefully. The snow pressing against the house made the den even cosier than usual. Sitting here listening to Aunt Florence's rich, reassuring voice was like being on an island. An island of safety in a world of dangers — Mick, and having to leave Canada. He closed his eyes and tried to will the evening to last forever.

But Mick finally had to be faced when school reopened on Thursday. The streets were still glutted with snow. Gavin kicked a hole in a snowbank as he waited at the usual corner for Tim and Roger. The money was safe in his mitt but he shivered inside. What if Mick wasn't satisfied?

"Hi, Gav." Tim threw a soft snowball at Gavin's stomach. "I was thinking about Mick." While they were shovelling together yesterday Gavin had told his friends all about the bully's threat.

"What about him?"

"Why don't we ambush him with snowballs? From behind the school fence so he won't see us. Then you could keep your money."

Tim was always suggesting things like this. *He* was brave — but too impulsive. "That wouldn't do any good," Gavin told him. "It might put Mick off for a while but he'd still look for me later to get the money. And if he found out it was us he'd be even madder."

Tim looked disappointed. "I guess so. Jeepers, why are people *like* Mick? Mean like him . . ."

Gavin shuddered. "He's even meaner than Charlie was." Charlie had been last year's bully, but now he went to Norah's high school.

"Remember when Charlie and his gang beat up your sister's friend just because he had a German last name?" said Tim.

"They cracked his rib!" said Gavin indignantly.

"I wonder if Charlie still picks on Bernard. Does your sister ever talk about him?"

"Bernard doesn't live in Toronto any more," said Gavin. "He and his mother moved back to

Kitchener." Gavin remembered how Bernard had always been nice to him. He could have told *him* about Mick.

Roger joined them, out of breath from running. "Sorry I'm late. Mum couldn't get out of bed and I had to make breakfast." As usual Roger looked worried. His mother had a bad back and his father, an officer in the navy, was fighting overseas. Roger was the only child — sometimes he even had to do the grocery shopping.

"What were you talking about?" he asked, as they started walking the remaining two blocks to school.

"Mick," sighed Gavin.

"Oh, him." Roger looked even more worried. "I just saw him."

The other two stared at him. "Where?"

"Hanging around by the store. He was making a kid in grade three eat some snow that had dog pee on it."

"He's such a creep!" cried Tim. "He's like a Nazi."

"A nasty Nazi," said Roger quietly.

Tim grinned. "Mick's a *nasty Nazi* . . . Mick's a *nasty Nazi* . . ." He and Gavin and Roger goose-stepped along the snowy sidewalk as they continued the chant. But not too loud, in case Mick was lurking nearby.

Gavin felt braver now that both of his friends were with him. Norah called them "The Three Musketeers" and they often pretended they were. They'd been friends since grade one.

Tim Flanagan was the middle one of six. He was round and emotional, but despite his frequent outbursts, he never let anything bother him for long — except for being hungry, which he always was.

Skinny Roger, on the other hand, appeared calm and quiet, but he constantly picked at the skin on his fingers and usually had an anxious frown on his face. "That Hewitt boy looks like a little old man," Aunt Florence said. Roger got high marks in all his subjects but after each report card he always said they could have been higher.

Three was a perfect number for games. Besides the Three Musketeers, they often played they were Sir Launcelot, Sir Galahad and Sir Gawaine, or the army, the navy and the air force. Gavin was the best at making things up, Roger knew the most facts, and Tim was the most daring.

"Should we stay with you while you give Mick the money?" asked Tim as they approached Prince Edward School.

If only they could; but Gavin shook his head. "Mick wouldn't like it if he knew I'd told you."

"Then we'll hide behind the fence. Come on, Rog!"

"No snowballs!" Gavin called after them. He watched them push through the excited crowd of kids playing in the snow. Then he went up to the flagpole — no Mick. He stood there alone for a long time, wishing he could be invisible like the Shadow.

"Hi, Gavin." Eleanor Austen came up to him.

"Hi, Eleanor." Gavin forgot his fear for a moment as he smiled at her. Eleanor was even smarter than Roger, and she was the prettiest girl in his class. Her eyelashes were so long she could balance eraser crumbs on them; last year she'd demonstrated. This morning her cheeks were the same colour as her red tam; her long brown braids hung in neat polished ropes from under it.

Some girls were unbearable. Like Lucy Smith. She was a grade ahead of Gavin and also a war guest, from the same English village as him and Norah. She and her sister and brother, Dulcie and Derek, had come over on the same ship. Now Derek had gone back to England to join the army, but Lucy and Dulcie still lived a few blocks away from the Ogilvies', at Reverend and Mrs Milne's.

Lucy acted as if she owned Gavin, bossing him in front of his friends. And Daphne Worsley, Paige's youngest sister, was even worse; Aunt Florence called her "a holy terror." At least Daphne went to a different school.

Eleanor, however, was *interesting*. She wrote dramatic stories, which she sometimes read aloud in class. And instead of a dog or a cat she had a pet monkey called Kilroy, which she had once brought to school.

Eleanor looked at Gavin urgently. "Quick!" she whispered. "They dared me to kiss you! So I'm just going to pretend, okay?" She smacked the air in front of his cheek, then rushed back to her friends watching from the girls' playground.

Gavin did what was expected of him. "Yech!" he cried, pretending to wipe off the kiss. The girls giggled.

Gavin's cheeks burned as much as Eleanor's had. Girls often dared each other to kiss him — him, Jamie and George, whom they had decided were the best-looking boys in grade five. Gavin had never liked it — but it had never been Eleanor before. He almost wished she hadn't just pretended.

A teacher came out and rang the first bell. The snowball fights stopped and everyone began to line up at the boys' and girls' entrances.

Where was Mick? Gavin was just about to dash into school when a rough voice behind him snarled, "Hand it over, Stoakes."

Gavin tore off his mitt and held up the red two-dollar bill. He was ashamed at how much his hand trembled. Mick grabbed the bill.

"Okay. You're safe. For now. . ." Both of them ran to their classrooms.

"Did you do it?" Tim whispered to Gavin, as they stood beside each other during "God Save the King."

Gavin nodded, trying to catch his breath. "But now I wish I hadn't. It's so unfair that he gets away with it!"

"At least you won't get beaten up," said Tim.

Mrs Moss directed one of her piercing glances at them. They clamped their mouths closed, then opened them again to chant "The Lord's Prayer."

"Any more talking, Tim and Gavin, and you'll be visiting with me after school today. Do you understand?" the teacher said after roll-call.

"Yes, Mrs Moss," they murmured. Mrs Moss was a new teacher this year and they still weren't sure whether to rate her as "nice" or "mean." She smiled more than "Sourpuss Liers," whom she'd replaced, but she was also strict; she always meant what she said.

"Now, because we had no school for the last two days, I wonder how many of you remembered to bring your quarters . . ."

Gavin had been so busy worrying about the money for Mick, he'd forgotten his war savings stamp money. He watched as some of the pupils exchanged their quarters for a stamp. They were allowed to paste it on one of the squares drawn over the large cartoon drawing of Hitler's face. Since September they had covered up almost half of it.

"There!" said Mrs Moss. "The rest of you please bring your money tomorrow. Now . . . I wonder if by any chance anyone has any news for this morning?" She looked mischievous; of course, *everyone* had stories about the blizzard.

Mrs Moss let six pupils recount their adventures of being stuck, looking for milk and bread, and shovelling people out. Gavin didn't contribute; he was still seething over the injustice of Mick. It was much easier to feel revengeful now that he was safe.

"I'm sure that many people were very grateful to you for helping," said Mrs Moss. "And now *I* have some news. You've probably noticed that Colin Porter hasn't been here this week. He and his sister Rose have returned to England. I just found out that they sailed last weekend."

The room buzzed as everyone turned around to stare at Colin's empty desk. But because Colin had been a prig and a tattle-tale, no one looked upset.

During arithmetic Gavin bent over his workbook, but he wasn't thinking about addition. He and Colin had been the last war guests in grade five. In grade one there had been three others in his class, but in the past two years they had all returned.

"Are you daydreaming again, Gavin?" asked Mrs Moss.

Gavin tried to concentrate. They were supposed to add a long column of three-figured numbers. He had always found it hard to think of numbers as just numbers. In grade one he had decided that some numbers were male and some female, and that each had a definite personality. He still couldn't help thinking of Six as a prissy woman who didn't like being next to pompous Nine. So how could he add them up?

They had to hand in their workbooks while Gavin was settling an argument between Three, a howling little girl, and Ten, a wise old man. That meant he'd have to stay in at recess tomorrow to finish it.

Next was a spelling test. Gavin waited for the monitors to fill his inkwell, rattling the little silver lid confidently. He'd had two extra evenings to study his speller and got every word right.

"When do you think *you'll* have to go back to England, Gav?" Roger asked him at recess. His dark eyes looked worried again.

"Not for a long time!" said Gavin hastily. "Not

until the war's over. That's what the social worker told us last month. Our parents don't think it will be safe until then. There's a new kind of bomb and lots of them fall over Kent."

"*Flying* bombs!" said Tim eagerly. "I know about those. I saw them on a newsreel."

"Maybe Colin will see a flying bomb," said Roger. "I bet he'll be scared."

Tim gave Gavin a friendly shove. "I hope the war is *never* over, Gav! Then you'll never have to leave Canada."

"But then my father wouldn't come back!" protested Roger.

"Oh yeah. Sorry, Rog."

"Let's stop talking about the war," said Gavin desperately. "Want to build a snow fort after school?"

III

Neither Calm
nor Bright

Gavin and Tim and Roger were careful to stay out of Mick's way for the rest of the term. Then the Christmas holidays started and they were free from worrying about him for a while.

Now there was lots of time to play in the huge amount of snow that still covered the ground. The three friends tobogganed, made snow forts and joined the highly organized snowball fights in the school playground. But as Christmas Day approached, Gavin became more and more uneasy.

"What's wrong with you, Gav?" Tim asked him. "You haven't been listening! I said, I *think* I'm getting a chemistry set. How about you? You always get such keen stuff."

Gavin couldn't explain how everything was

different this year. Although no one could bear to talk about it, everyone in the Ogilvie household was aware that this was Gavin and Norah's last Christmas in Canada. It was hard to ignore the sad looks he kept getting, not only from Aunt Florence, Aunt Mary and Hanny, but from the five Montreal relatives who'd come to stay — "cousins" and "aunts and uncles" that he knew from Gairloch, the island they went to in Muskoka every summer.

On Christmas Eve afternoon Gavin sat in the living room having a game of checkers with Uncle Reg. Aunt Florence had managed to find a tree. It was much spindlier than usual but it still glittered with the same glass balls and bubble lights that covered it every year. The same angel perched on top and the usual hill of presents buried its lower branches. Gavin kept glancing at the tree, taking whiffs of its piney smell for reassurance.

Uncle Reg reached down and fondled one of Bosley's ears. "Well, Boz, do you miss me?" Bosley raised one paw and shook hands politely, but then he pushed under the table and put his head in Gavin's lap.

"He certainly prefers *you* now," chuckled Uncle Reg. He jumped his checker over one of Gavin's, then looked up, unusually serious. "Gavin, I want you to know that when you have to return to England I would give Bosley to you for good — if he was allowed to go."

A flash of hope filled Gavin. "*Is* he?"

"I'm afraid not, son." The old man looked sorrowful. "I even made inquiries. Dogs aren't allowed into Britain without going into quarantine for months. We couldn't do that to Boz."

"No," agreed Gavin sadly. "He'd be too lonely." He swallowed hard. "I know I have to give him up, Uncle Reg. You said that when you lent him to me. It's okay."

Uncle Reg smiled at him. "You're a brave boy." Then he sighed. "I think Florence was probably right. I shouldn't have given Bosley to you in the first place. I should have realized how hard it was going to be when the time came for you to go back."

"But I'm *glad* you gave him — lent him — to me! He's one of my best friends!" Then Gavin couldn't help sniffling.

Uncle Reg handed him a large, soft handkerchief, looking as if he were going to cry too. "I promise you I'll take very good care of him and I'll always think of him as *your* dog — as if you've lent him to *me*! I'll send you reports and pictures of him."

Gavin blew his nose, handed back the handkerchief and tried to smile. Then Uncle Reg might stop talking about Bosley.

"I have a perfect word for charades this year," chuckled Uncle Reg. "Let's try to get on the same team." Gavin cheered up as Uncle Reg told him how he planned to use the word to trick Aunt Florence.

That evening a crowd of visitors filled the living room. At one end the teen-agers gathered: Aunt Florence's great-nieces, Flo and Janet, Paige, Paige's sister Barbara, Dulcie and Norah. They shrieked with laughter as Paige, the tallest and wildest, imitated the headmistress at her girls' school. The adults sat with their drinks and cigarettes at the other end of the room, praising Uncle Reg for managing to get a bottle of rye.

Gavin was stuck with Daphne and Lucy. He slouched between them while they chattered about tomorrow morning.

"I always get up at five o'clock and open my stocking," declared Daphne, spitting out crumbs of shortbread as she spoke. "They make me go back to bed until seven, but then we *run* downstairs and rip open all the presents."

Lucy looked prim. "*We* have to wait until Uncle Cedric gets back from early service, then we have to get dressed and have breakfast before we have the tree. Then we go to church. That's exactly how we did it in England."

Daphne pinched Gavin's leg. "Ouch!" he protested. "I wish you wouldn't always do that, Daphne."

"I bet you'll miss my pinches when you go back to England," she smirked.

"That'll be the only good part about going back," he retorted.

"But don't you *want* to go back, Gavin?" Lucy asked him. "I can hardly wait to see my parents again! I'll miss Canada and the Milnes, of course, but England is our *real* home."

Everything Lucy said always sounded like something she was copying from the grown-ups. Gavin shrugged. Daphne pinched him again and he got up indignantly.

If only the Montreal cousins who were his age — Peter and Ross and Sally — had come this year. He found a chair in a corner and curled up in it, thinking of all the good times he had with those three at Gairloch every summer. But if the war was over by next summer — and everyone seemed to think it would be — he wouldn't be in Canada.

In August Norah and Gavin had walked around the island by themselves on the morning they'd left. Norah had been in tears. "This is going to be the hardest part of Canada to give up," she said, gazing greedily at every rock and tree. "It's probably the last time we'll ever be here." Gavin hadn't believed her. Now he did.

And if he would probably be back in England this summer, that meant he'd be there for sure by next Christmas . . . Gavin glanced at the brown paper parcel from his parents under the tree. It always looked so plain compared to the other presents in their bright paper and ribbon. Next Christmas, when he and Norah were with their parents, would *all* their presents be wrapped in plain brown paper?

Uncle Reg went over to the piano and everyone gathered around to sing carols. Gavin tried to make himself feel Christmassy, especially when they sang "Good King Wenceslas." It had become a family tradition for Uncle Reg and Gavin to sing the parts of the king and the page. Usually this was Gavin's favourite part of Christmas Eve, imagining himself following a king "through the rude wind's wild lament / And the bitter weather."

Sire, the night is darker now,
And the wind grows stronger:
Fails my heart, I know not how,
I can go no longer

sang Gavin when it was his turn. But this year the song seemed unbearably sad, even after the king's reassuring answer.

"That was wonderful, pet!" Aunt Florence whispered. "You really made the words come alive!"

They had just begun "Silent Night" when all the lights in the house went out.

"Oh, *no*! Not on Christmas Eve!" someone cried.

The girls giggled in the darkness and Daphne pinched Gavin again. But soon one of the adults had found candles and the living room became a soft, flickering cave.

"Let's carry on," said Uncle Reg. "I can see well enough."

"All is calm, all is bright," they sang.

"It certainly isn't calm and bright tonight!" laughed one of the aunts at the end.

The family sat down and sipped eggnog. Gavin snuggled up against Aunt Florence. In the last few years Toronto had often had power failures. He liked the way the house seemed to shrink around him, enclosing him in a safe cocoon.

"This is what it must be like all the time in England," said Aunt Mary.

"*I* remember," said Dulcie. "We had to cover

every inch of the window with black curtains. People came around and inspected to make sure not one chink of light showed."

"Well, soon they won't have to do that any more," said Mr Worsley. "Just like that song — what is it?"

"When the Lights Go On Again," said Lucy importantly. "We sing it in school."

"But then you'll all have to go back," said Janet. She clutched Norah's arm as if she'd never let her go.

That made everyone look sadly again at Norah, Gavin, Dulcie and Lucy. Gavin shivered. He *never* wanted the lights to go on.

Christmas morning was different too. Usually Peter and Ross shared Gavin's room and they inspected the stockings on the ends of their beds together. This year he opened his stocking all by himself. After he had spread everything out on his bed — a cap gun, pencils, comics, a package of Chiclets, two rolls of Lifesavers, notepaper, and an orange in the toe — he put it all back carefully in the stocking and went up to the tower. There he spilled it out again with Norah, Janet and Flo.

As in Lucy's house they had to get dressed and eat breakfast before they had the tree. Gavin always relished the delicious suspense while they waited for the adults to finish. This year, at least that part was the same. As he waited on the stairs in front of the closed living-room door he felt Christmassy for the first time.

But when they were finally allowed to dash in, he tried to hide his disappointment. Usually there was something large under the tree for him: one year it had been skis, another year a new bike. But this Christmas all his presents were wrapped — and small.

The presents themselves were okay: a baseball glove, several airplane models and some books he had wanted. But he'd hoped for a new hockey stick. And his present from Aunt Florence was baffling: two tiny, engraved gold circles lying on cotton batting in a small blue box.

"They're much too old for you, pet," said Aunt Florence. "But they're very valuable and I want you to keep them safe until you're grown up. They belonged to my husband."

Aunt Florence looked so proud he couldn't hurt her feelings by asking what the strange objects were. "Thank you very much," he said. "I'll take good care of them."

"I'm sorry that all your presents are so small, sweetness," she said. "But we didn't want to give you anything this year that you couldn't take home with you." Then her strong face crumpled.

So that was why. Gavin tried to be grateful. After all, he already had plenty of stuff — more than most boys his age. It wasn't that he didn't like what he'd received; it was just the *change*.

Norah, too, got something that was old, but at least you could tell what it was: a short string of pearls.

"They were given to me when I was your age," smiled Aunt Mary.

"They're real, so take good care of them," warned Aunt Florence.

"I will. *Thank* you!" Norah tried on the pearls while Janet admired them.

At ten o'clock they all gathered around the radio for the King's Christmas message. The young people squirmed but the adults listened intently.

"We do not know what awaits us when we open the door of 1945 . . ." said the hesitant, English voice. "The darkness daily grows less and less. The lamps which the Germans put out all over Europe, first in 1914 and then in 1939, are being slowly rekindled. Already we can see some of them beginning to shine through the fog of war that still shrouds so many lands."

"That was his best speech yet," said Aunt Dorothy at the end, wiping her eyes.

"And hasn't his voice improved! He never stutters any more," said Aunt Florence approvingly — as if King George VI were her personal responsibility.

While the family was walking along the snowy sidewalks to church, Gavin lingered behind the adults with Norah.

"You know those little gold things I got," he muttered. "What *are* they?"

"They're cuff-links, silly! You use them to keep your cuffs together."

"But I have buttons on my cuffs!"

"Later you'll just have holes, and then you'll use cuff-links. Look at Uncle Reg's shirtsleeves."

Gavin sneaked a look at them during church.

Sure enough, Uncle Reg's sleeves were held shut with two gold circles, just like his. He sighed. What a boring present.

Beside him Norah ran her fingers along her pearls. "Isn't it strange to think that next Christmas morning we'll be in church in Ringden?" she whispered, as Reverend Milne talked about the growing possibility of world peace.

Gavin nodded miserably. Norah, however, looked eager, not miserable. That made him feel even more alone.

After church they had Christmas dinner. Hanny roasted a goose and everyone commented on how it was just as good as a turkey. Gavin ate as much as he could to fill up the empty space inside him.

When the meal was over Uncle Reg and Uncle Barclay fell asleep in front of the living-room fire, still wearing the paper hats from their crackers. Hanny went home to her husband, and the aunts and cousins did the dishes. On other Christmases this was the time of day when Gavin and the younger cousins played with their new toys. This year he wandered into the living room, wondering what to do. He sat down and opened up one of his new books. It was called *Rabbit Hill* and it looked good, but he couldn't concentrate. The uncles snored gently. He could hear the women singing "We all want figgy pudding" in the kitchen. He had offered to help, but they'd shooed him out.

Finally the dishes were done and the others came into the living room, teasing the uncles as always for falling asleep. Flo, the oldest cousin, stretched out her legs and sighed. "What a nice break. I wish I didn't have to go back tomorrow." She was in the RCAF and only had two days' leave.

"I wonder what Andrew's doing right now?" said her younger sister, Janet.

"His mother said his last letter was dated October," said Aunt Dorothy. "All we know is that he's somewhere in Italy."

"I hope he got my parcel," said Janet. "I knit him some socks."

"We sent him some food and books but so many parcels don't seem to ever reach him," sighed Aunt Mary.

"I hope you girls are all writing to Andrew regularly," said Aunt Florence.

"I do — every month," said Flo.

"I write *twice* a month," boasted Janet.

"Do you hear that, Norah? Norah says she doesn't need to write to Andrew because she's not related to him," sniffed Aunt Florence. "But the dear boy needs all the letters he can get to keep up his spirits."

Norah ignored Aunt Florence's disapproving frown. Gavin was careful not to look at his sister. He knew that, ever since Andrew had spent the summer before last with them at Gairloch, Norah had been writing secretly to him. He occasionally wrote back, to Paige's address.

Gavin also knew that Norah was in love with Andrew. She'd told him that one night after Andrew had gone to fight overseas and he'd found her in tears.

"Don't tell anyone," she'd said. "They'll tease me and say I'm too young. But I won't be too young when he comes back."

If he came back. That was why everyone looked so grave at the mention of his name, and why Norah always snatched the paper and scanned the casualty lists before the aunts saw it. Whenever Gavin watched a newsreel showing dead soldiers he closed his eyes in case one of them was Andrew.

Gavin squirmed. Norah wasn't quite fifteen. She wasn't even allowed to date. If the war was over soon, surely she would still be too young for Andrew. Surely she couldn't get *married* — could she?

When the family switched from Andrew to news of other relatives Gavin let himself glance at Norah. She was staring into the fire dreamily. She looked as grown-up as Flo, he realized with alarm. Aunt Florence had let her wear lipstick and stockings and her long hair was carefully curled at the ends. Did Norah have to change along with everything else?

Norah didn't look very grown-up after supper, as she helped her team act out the first syllable in their word for charades. She and Aunt Mary huffed and puffed, their hair in their eyes, as they jumped around the room with their feet together, clutching the sides of their dresses.

"Can-can!"

"Hop!"

"Rabbit!"

"Give up . . ." gasped Norah. "We can't do this forever. And it's only one syllable!"

"I know!" said Janet. It's a sack race! *Sack*!"

"Right!" laughed Aunt Mary, collapsing on a chair.

But no one could guess the next two syllables. First Aunt Dorothy and Flo dressed as tramps, then everyone on the team drank something and held their imaginary glasses up to their ears. For the whole word they carried in Norah, her hands and feet tied up, and pretended to burn her on a fire.

"Aha!" said Aunt Florence. "Sacrifice!"

"You *always* guess," grumbled Flo.

"But what was the second syllable?" asked Janet. "The third was 'ice,' but what were all those rags you were wearing? 'Riff'?"

"The first part of riff-raff!" said Flo, as the others groaned.

"Our turn," said Uncle Reg. "For our first word I want to change things a bit. We'll do the whole word at once, with no syllables. And only Gavin and I will know what the word is."

"But why can't the rest of your team know?" demanded Aunt Florence.

"You'll see," said Uncle Reg. He took the dressing-gown belts that had been used to tie up Norah and formed them into a figure eight on the rug. "Now, Florence, you sit down in one circle facing outwards, and, Barclay, you sit in the other."

"This sounds like one of your tricks, Reg," said Aunt Florence.

"It's just charades, Florence. Will you please sit down?"

Finally she lowered her large rear into one of the circles. Uncle Barclay stoically sat down in the other.

"That's the word," grinned Gavin. "It has four syllables."

Everyone tried half-hearted guesses but no one came near.

"Really, Reg, I feel very foolish sitting here," complained Aunt Florence.

"Not as foolish as you're about to feel!" smiled her brother. "Give up?" Everyone nodded. "Tell them, Gavin."

"Assassinate!" crowed Gavin. The uproar that followed — even Aunt Florence laughed — made Gavin forget for the only time that this was his last Christmas in Canada.

The visiting relatives caught the train back to Montreal on Boxing Day. Gavin spent the morning at Roger's, but after lunch he had to stay in to write his thank-you notes. He sat at the desk in the study, staring at the list Aunt Florence had given him and swinging his legs. Bosley snoozed at his feet. Writing thank-yous was so tedious, but Aunt Florence always insisted it be done right away.

Finally he dipped his pen into the inkwell and began the first letter on the list. "Dear Mum and Dad. Thank you for the wooden truck and the hat. I like them very much." He put down his pen. Didn't his parents realize that he was much too old for

wooden toys and that he already had plenty of hats?
Then he wiggled with guilt. He knew that Dad had
carved the truck and Mum had knit the hat. Their
letters often said how impossible it was to find new
toys in England. Norah's eyes had filled with tears
when she'd unwrapped the homemade blouse Mum
had sewn her. Gavin wished they wouldn't send
anything at all — then he wouldn't have to feel so
ungrateful.

He closed his eyes and tried to remember his
real family, but their faces were blank. They were
simply names: Mum, Dad and Grandad; his sister
Muriel, her husband, Barry, and their new baby;
and his other sister, Tibby. They were like distant
relatives he never saw, as distant as a cousin of
Aunt Florence's in Manitoba, who always sent
him a small Christmas present, but whom he'd
never met.

He picked up his pen and finished the letter,
describing Christmas Day and his other presents.
Then he scribbled his other notes as quickly as he
could to get them over with.

Finally he blotted the last envelope. He piled
them on the hall table and went up to his room to
read. But Bosley wouldn't stay with him. He kept
going out of the bedroom, then coming back to
Gavin and whining.

"What's the matter, boy? You've just *been* out."

He got up and followed the dog into the
upstairs hall. Bosley was standing at the half-open
door of Aunt Florence's room. He looked back
anxiously at Gavin.

Gavin listened for a moment. Surely it couldn't be . . . crying. Not Aunt Florence. She *never* cried.

But the sound was unmistakable. He peeked through the crack of the door and saw Aunt Florence sitting at her dressing table. Her back was towards him and her shoulders were shaking. One hand clutched the woven paper mat he'd made for her in school. He'd written "Merry Christmas to Aunt Florence from Gavin" on it in his best handwriting.

Gavin scurried back to his room. Aunt Florence wasn't *ever* supposed to cry! He read his book intently, letting the story carry him away from her weeping.

IV

An Ordinary Winter

Nineteen forty-five began with the coldest January Toronto had had in twenty-five years. Whenever Gavin went outside he had to wear extra clothes: long underwear, another pair of mitts, a fleece-lined leather cap with flaps, and a scarf tied over his mouth and nose. The scarf kept falling down, freezing into a hard woolly clump where his mouth had wetted it.

At least the cold weather slowed down Mick. No one stood still long enough for him to threaten, and many recesses were spent indoors, where teachers supervised them more than usual.

Every morning Mrs Moss talked about how the Germans were being cornered by the Allies — but still the war didn't end. Aunt Florence stopped mentioning Gavin and Norah's return to England. Gavin decided to pretend it wasn't going to happen.

The winter days and months slipped by like beads on a string — orderly and normal. Gavin threw himself into his activities in a sort of dream.

The city streets were still so blocked with snow that the scrap-paper pick-ups were halted. Instead the schools had a competition to see which one could collect the most paper. Gavin and Tim and Roger hauled paper to the schoolyard on their toboggans, then bundled and stacked it until their arms ached. The piles in the schoolyard grew and grew. Mr Evans, the principal, told them proudly that even though they hadn't won, Prince Edward School had collected several tons of paper.

Gavin and Tim and Roger went downtown to see the helicopter that was being exhibited in Simpson's department store. If you brought some war savings stamps with you, you were allowed to climb inside and sit at the controls.

Gavin got three more badges in Cubs and two goals in hockey. Roger turned eleven, and Tim ate so much at his party that he threw up all over the rug and was sent home in disgrace. Gavin and Tim were caught chewing gum by Mr Evans. He made them stay after school and scrape off enough gum from under the desks to fill up a piece of paper each.

On February 2 the groundhog saw his shadow. Tim's parents took him and Gavin to the Ice Follies. The Ogilvie household celebrated Norah's fifteenth birthday by all going to see *Blithe Spirit* at the Royal Alexandra Theatre.

Mick got the strap again, for beating up Russell Jones in the washroom. A teacher had been walking by and heard the commotion.

Norah had an argument with Aunt Florence about staying out late at the new canteen that had opened for teen-agers. "*Everyone stays* until mid-night!" she protested, but Aunt Florence just said, "Fiddlesticks! You're not everyone and I want you home by ten-thirty."

Norah won first prize in her school speech contest. The topic was "My Hero." Norah spoke clearly and fervently about Amelia Earhart, the first woman to fly an airplane across the Atlantic Ocean.

"You were very good, my dear," said Aunt Florence.

"You were wonderful!" cried Aunt Mary. "I never could have stood up in front of all those people when I was your age. And what a fascinating woman! Why did you choose her?"

"Miss Gleeson at the library gave me a book about her." Norah grinned, stroking her trophy. "Maybe I'll be a pilot too, one day."

"A pilot!" spluttered Aunt Florence. "Don't be absurd, Norah." But Norah looked thoughtful.

Three more girls in grade five kissed Gavin. Jamie and George kept getting kissed too. Then Jamie tattled and Mrs Moss told the girls they had to stop "all this kissing nonsense."

Gavin got fourteen valentines — the same as the number of girls in his class. Roger and Tim teased him and he pretended to despise the valentines. But he went through them all at home, trying to guess which one was Eleanor's.

One Saturday evening a boy turned up at the Ogilvies' front door, asked for Norah, and was ushered into the hall.

"This is — um — Michael Carey," Norah told Aunt Florence.

Michael shook hands nervously as Aunt Florence inspected him. Gavin sneaked a look at him and Norah as they sat together in the living room. Both had flushed faces and neither spoke much. Norah seemed relieved when Michael left half an hour later.

"Is he your boy friend?" Gavin asked her.

"No! He's just a boy in my class," muttered Norah.

Aunt Florence came into the hall. "He seems like a presentable young man, Norah. I know his grandmother." She smiled. "Now that you're fifteen, my dear, I will allow you to go out with boys, as long as I meet them first."

"Thanks, but I don't *want* to date," retorted Norah.

"Very well . . . it's up to you, of course." Aunt Florence walked away huffily; she didn't like having her favours refused.

"Why don't you want to date?" asked Gavin. "You do other things with boys."

Norah lifted her chin proudly. "I like dancing with boys at the canteen and I like talking to them when we go to Murray's for a milkshake. But I refuse to be attached to anyone! There's only one person I'm interested in. Michael and the other boys in my school can never come up to *him*. But don't forget, Gavin, that's a secret."

"I know. Norah . . ."

"Mmm?" Norah looked dreamy.

"Do you – uhh – do you think ten is too young to like girls? I mean for a boy." The minute he said that he regretted it. What if she teased him?

But Norah regarded him seriously. "Nope. If you like someone, you like them. It doesn't matter how old you are." She took his hand. "Come on — I'll teach you how to play crib."

In March the snow finally melted. Gavin and Tim and Roger spent most of their after-school time fixing up their fort in the ravine behind the Ogilvies' house. Bosley tried to help by chasing away squirrels.

Mick cornered Roger one afternoon in the ravine. He forced him to take off all his clothes and ran away with them, leaving Roger shivering and crying in the fort.

When the others found him there, Gavin raced up the hill to the house to get some of his clothes while Tim wrapped Roger in his jacket.

"We *should* tell on Mick!" said Gavin when he'd come back. He turned pale at the thought of his friend's ordeal. "He shouldn't get away with this!"

"No!" cried Roger. "The more he's punished the worse he gets!"

"He should be *expelled*," said Tim.

"That's the only solution," said Roger. "But how can we be sure Mr Evans *would* expel him?

He's never expelled anyone before." He looked down at the sleeves of Gavin's sweater dangling below his wrists. "What am I going to say to my mother? That jacket was brand new! I'll have to make something up so *she* won't tell."

"From now on we have to stick together all the time," said Gavin.

"All for one and one for all!" cried Tim. But Roger just sat on a log looking wretched.

The weather became warmer and warmer. The grown-ups smiled and said it was a good omen. Tulip bulbs sent green swords up through the damp earth, and Aunt Mary ordered seeds for this year's Victory Garden. In school they kept singing "When the lights go on again/All over the world." But all over the world the war carried on.

V

The Telegram

"See ya later, alligator," called Tim as the three of them parted at the corner.

"After a while, crocodile," Gavin answered.

"Don't forget your glove," came Roger's distant cry. They were meeting again in twenty minutes to play baseball.

Gavin peeled off his jacket as he walked home. The soft spring air was almost hot. His shoes felt wonderfully light on the bare sidewalk, after trudging along it in galoshes all winter.

He turned into Sir Launcelot, rescuing a princess from a dragon. The princess looked just like Eleanor. He whacked a bush with a stick as the dragon's head fell off.

"Oh, Sir Launcelot, you are the bravest knight in the kingdom!" the princess cried. A passing woman smiled at him and Gavin realized he'd been muttering to himself.

"Wave, Boz!" he cried as he neared the end of his block. The dog lifted his paw in a comical salute, then hurtled towards Gavin, jumped all over him and licked his face. He led Gavin the rest of the way to the Ogilvies', his tail beating. The two of them raced up the stairs and into the hall. Gavin stopped to check the mail.

A letter for him! He tore it open. Good — his Mysto-Snapper Membership Badge for Orphan Annie's Secret Guard had arrived. Tim had got his two days ago. Gavin crammed it back into the envelope. Then he noticed something else lying on the hall table.

A yellow envelope. The kind of envelope a telegram came in.

Everyone knew what a telegram meant. Gloria Pendleton's family had received one last year when her father had been killed in France.

Bosley whined and looked anxious, the same way he had when they heard Aunt Florence crying. Now Gavin realized that, again, someone was crying. The sound came from the den. Aunt Mary, he guessed, listening hard.

"No-o-o . . ." she wailed. Then Norah said, "It's not true! I just can't believe it's *true!*" Aunt Florence's voice, broken and bitter, croaked, "What a waste. What a *wicked wicked* waste."

Hanny came out of the kitchen. At the sight of Gavin she sobbed and held up her apron to her red, swollen eyes.

"What's wrong?" said Gavin. "What happened?"

"I can't bear to tell you. Go into the den. They're all in there." She ran back to the kitchen, crying even louder.

Andrew . . . It must be Andrew.

Gavin thought of Andrew's laughing face two summers ago when he'd taken them all sailing. Then he thought of Norah. Tears formed in his eyes.

He should go straight into the den and join them, but his feet seemed stuck to the floor. He stood there and stared at the yellow envelope. The silver bowl of roses on the hall table gave off a heavy, dizzying smell.

Sir Launcelot would be brave. *He* wouldn't cry; he would go and comfort his sister. Gavin took a deep breath and walked into the den.

Norah was sitting stiffly on the edge of the chesterfield. When she saw him she winced as if she'd been stabbed. Her eyes were filled with such acute pain he had to look away. This was how much she had loved Andrew.

"I can't tell him," she whispered.

"*I'll* tell him," said Aunt Florence. "Come here, sweetness." She sat down and held out her arms. Gavin walked slowly towards her. It was just like the day he'd entered this room for the first time and Aunt Florence had summoned him into the protection of her strong embrace.

He stood in front of her. Her firm hands gripped both his shoulders while she spoke. On the small table beside her chair lay the telegram, but he couldn't see the print clearly.

"Gavin, I have something terrible to tell you. You're going to have to be very brave."

"Yes, Aunt Florence," said Gavin. "Is it Andrew?"

"Andrew!" She looked bewildered for a second, then let go of his shoulders and sighed heavily. "No, pet. It's not Andrew. It's — it's your mother and father. They've been killed by a flying bomb in England."

He couldn't have heard her properly. He stared, then finally whispered, "Killed?" Aunt Mary began sobbing again.

"Yes, pet," said Aunt Florence gently. "Your grandfather sent us a telegram. Do you want to read it?"

Gavin took the telegram from her. For a few seconds the black letters danced against the yellow background, then were still.

REGRET MY DAUGHTER AND SON-IN-LAW KILLED BY V-1 STOP PLEASE TELL CHILDREN AND CONVEY OUR LOVE AND SORROW STOP LETTER FOLLOWING JAMES LOGGIN.

Gavin handed it back. "Do you understand, pet?" Aunt Florence asked him.

"Yes," he whispered. Aunt Florence pulled him onto her knee as if he were five again. He felt babyish, perching there, but he couldn't protest.

"*Damn* this war!" sobbed Aunt Mary. "Damn,

damn, *damn!* Why should such a monstrous thing happen to two innocent children?" Gavin gaped at her. Aunt Mary *never* used words like that!

He slid off Aunt Florence's lap, but she kept her arm around him. Norah still sat in her frozen position; he couldn't look at her face again. Aunt Mary was beside her, but she seemed afraid to touch her.

Hanny brought in a tray of tea. "You and Norah have some too," she urged them. "I made it good and sweet — who cares about rationing at a time like this?" She sat down with them while the adults talked in low, shocked voices.

My mother and father are *dead*, Gavin said to himself, sipping the hot sugary liquid. He tried to make himself cry.

"I think you two should go up to Norah's room," said Aunt Florence, when they'd finished their tea. "I'm sure you want to be alone together. We'll call you for dinner."

Gavin trudged up the stairs after Norah, thinking regretfully of Tim and Roger waiting for him in the park.

Norah sat on the window-seat in the tower, staring at nothing. Gavin tried to think of something to say.

"Is it really true, Gavin?" She kept her eyes away from him.

Gavin shivered at how strange her voice sounded. "It must be," he said carefully. "The telegram said so."

"But maybe . . . maybe it's the wrong family! Maybe they sent it to the wrong address!"

"It had our grandfather's name on it."

"Yes. So it must be true," she said dully.

She was quiet for a long time. So was Gavin. Bosley had followed them to the tower. He jumped up beside Norah and rested his head on her knee.

Finally Norah broke the silence. "I *knew* it."

"What do you mean?"

"I knew they'd be killed," she said slowly. Her voice was singsongy and faraway. "I've had a nightmare about it for years — I never told you. A nightmare that their house was bombed and they were all killed. Except *Grandad* isn't dead. That's right, isn't it?" she asked, as if she were asking herself, not him. "He sent the telegram, so he can't be dead. That's the only thing that's different from my dream. And listen to this, Gavin." She twisted a corner of the curtain in her hands and her voice became shrill. "I dreamt it again *two nights ago*. I hadn't had the dream for almost a year, but then I did. Maybe that's the day it happened! Maybe — "

"Stop it, Norah!" Gavin put his hands on her shoulders and shook her hard. "I don't think you should *talk* about your dream!"

She looked right at him for the first time — as if he'd woken her up. "Sorry, Gavin," she said softly. "I didn't mean to scare you." She sighed. "You're right. What's the use of talking about it *now*?" She picked up his hand. "Oh, Gavin . . . I just can't *believe* it! Can you?"

Gavin shook his head.

Norah went over to her bedside table and took out a letter from the drawer. She brought it back to the window-seat and gazed intently at it. "This is Dad's writing. The last letter from them before they died. Do you want me to read it to you?"

"If you want," whispered Gavin.

Norah began to read the letter. Gavin had already heard its contents, of course, when it arrived in February. His parents were full of excitement about the black-out finally beginning to be lifted in England: churches could let their stained-glass windows show and car headlights no longer had to be masked. The Home Guard was disbanded, so Dad could stay home in the evenings. "The world is getting brighter and soon you will be with us again," read Norah's quavering voice. "Best love to you both, D-Dad and Mum."

Norah began to shake. Then she erupted in tears. She threw herself on the window-seat's pillows as her body heaved and shuddered. "Oh Dad ... Mum ..."

Gavin clenched his fists, trying to stop the wave of fear that broke over him. "Don't cry, Norah," he said, patting her back as if she were Bosley. "Don't cry." Bosley tried to lick her.

But she kept on crying for a long time while Gavin sat awkwardly beside her. Then she raised her wet face. She stumbled into the bathroom and blew her nose loudly. "I'll tell you one thing, Gavin," she sniffed, coming to sit down again. "Wh-whatever — whatever happens to us, we'll always stick together. No one is going to s-separate us, all r-right?" Her body shook with dry sobs.

"Of course not!" said Gavin with surprise.

"What do you think *will* happen to us?" he added. A wonderful thought came to him. "Will we — will we stay in Canada now?"

"No, we won't!" Norah's anger froze her sobs. She looked so fierce that Gavin felt ashamed. "Don't *ever* think that! We're *English*! England is our home! We'll go back and live with Grandad, of course."

"Oh." So everything was the same. When the war was over he still had to go back to England.

Norah thumped the pillows. "I wish we knew more about how it happened! Then it would be easier to believe. Why didn't Grandad say more?" She sighed. "I guess we'll just have to wait for his letter."

"Why don't we phone him?"

"They — M-mum and Dad — didn't have a phone. And we don't even know if Grandad is in the house any more. We don't even know if the house is still *there* . . ." She picked up Dad's letter again. "I still can't believe it! I need to be alone, Gavin. Tell them I don't want any dinner, okay? We'll talk again in the morning. Will you be all right?"

Gavin nodded. He wasn't all right, but he could never tell her why. Not because he felt sad about his parents. Because he didn't feel anything at all.

Gavin and Norah stayed home from school for the rest of that week. Aunt Florence arranged a memorial service for Saturday. "They'll be having a funeral in England, of course, but *we* have to do something too. It's important for the children to go through a ritual," Gavin heard her say to Aunt Mary. Both of them seemed grateful to throw themselves into getting ready for the service.

Norah stalked around the house with puffy eyes, breaking into torrents of tears with no warning. The adults kept handing her fresh handkerchiefs and tried to comfort her. Gavin wished he could escape from her pain, but he forced himself to listen every time she wanted to talk.

"If only I'd *told* them!" she agonized.

"Told them what?"

"Told them about my dream! Then it might not have happened!"

Other times she talked about how she shouldn't have argued so much with her mother. "I was awful to Mum our last night at home," she moaned. "I hardly spoke to her, I was so mad they were sending us to Canada — and that was almost the last time I saw her!"

Gavin tried to comfort his sister, but his words bounced off her grief — as if Norah were enclosed in a box that shut him out.

Almost worse was how everyone in the family kept asking how *he* was. He muttered, "I'm okay," but they didn't seem to believe him. He knew they wanted him to cry. But however hard he tried, he couldn't.

If only he could go out and play with his friends as if this hadn't happened! Aunt Florence even suggested it, but Gavin didn't know what he'd say to them.

Instead he spent long hours in his room, making a difficult model or reading until his eyes stung. At least next week he'd be allowed to go back to school. But that would be different as well, he thought drearily. Now *everything* was different.

St Peter's Church was packed. Gavin sat in the front pew with Norah, the Ogilvies, Hanny and her husband, and Uncle Reg, who'd come to represent the Montreal relatives. He sneaked some looks behind him while they were singing "The Lord Is My Shepherd." Tim was there beside his parents, and Roger with his mother. He avoided their eyes. He also spotted Mrs Moss, Mr Evans, Paige and her family, and Dulcie and Lucy. Even Miss Gleeson, the public librarian whom Norah and Gavin had got to know over the years, was there.

Gavin tried to pay attention to when he was supposed to stand and sit and kneel. He tried not to think about musketeers or baseball or the new trick he was teaching Bosley.

"Let not your hearts be troubled," said Reverend Milne. He looked down at the front pew with such a concerned expression that Gavin flushed and hung his head.

The last hymn was "Abide With Me." Aunt Florence and Aunt Mary kept dabbing their eyes with their handkerchiefs. Norah didn't sing but held her head high. "She's being *so* brave," Gavin heard Hanny whisper to her husband.

"Where is death's sting / Where, grave, thy vic-tor-y . . ." Gavin shifted with impatience; what a *slow* hymn. Half the people in the church were weeping while the ponderous melody droned on. Gavin could feel the whole congregation's pity pressing against his back. Why did his parents have to go and die and put him through this?

A grave, dark-clothed crowd filled the Ogilvies' house after the service. Norah was safe in a corner; Paige and Dulcie and their sisters surrounded her protectively, warding off sympathetic adults. Gavin wasn't as lucky. He had to shake hands and say "thank you" again and again, as one person after another came up and said "I'm so sorry." Women kept glancing at him and wiping their eyes.

Tim and Roger approached with their parents. Gavin turned as crimson as if he'd been found out about something he'd done wrong. His friends looked just as embarrassed.

Tim's father put his hand on Gavin's head and Tim's mother hugged him wordlessly. Roger's mother clasped his hand and murmured something about "this terrible war." Then the three adults waited for Tim and Roger to say something.

"I'm sorry about your parents," mumbled Roger, his head down and his fingers scratching rapidly at the skin on his thumbs.

"Me too," said Tim. "Was it a V-1 or a V-2 bomb?"

"Tim!" cried his parents, pulling him away.

"He hasn't cried yet," Aunt Mary was telling Paige's mother. "We're not sure it's sunk in."

"He doesn't *have* to cry, Mary," said Aunt Florence. "He hardly remembers his parents. *I'm* much more of a mother to him now."

Gavin chewed on a sandwich, the crumbs sticking in his throat. Aunt Florence was the only one who understood.

VI

Try To Remember

On Monday Norah said she couldn't face school yet and no one made her go. Gavin, however, was out of the house as soon as he finished breakfast. He took his bike and didn't pause to wait at the corner for Tim and Roger.

After the bell he sat at his desk, lowering his flushed face, while Mrs Moss told him in front of the whole class how sorry they were. At recess all of grade five avoided him, as if he had some disease. At lunchtime Tim and Roger gave him clumsy smiles, then quickly bicycled away.

Finally Gavin couldn't stand it. After school he went up to Tim and Roger at the bike stands.

"Hi." He tried to smile nonchalantly, but his cheeks burned.

"Oh, hi, Gav," mumbled Roger.

"How are you?" added Tim.

"I'm all right. Look . . ." Gavin paused. Then he rushed out his words before he lost his nerve. "Look, let's just *forget* about my parents. I mean, not forget about them . . . but let's just act like before. Okay?"

"Okay!" said Tim. "Do you want to go to the fort? One wall needs fixing."

"Sure!" said Gavin.

"Uh-oh . . . Mick's standing over there by the corner of the school," whispered Roger.

Tim swung his leg across his bike. "Who cares? All for one and one for all!"

Gavin glanced at Mick. The bully was staring intensely, at *him*. He cycled fast to catch up with Tim and Roger.

All week teachers and some of the older girls came up to Gavin to say they were sorry. But now that he had his friends back he didn't mind as much. He was practised at smiling sadly and saying "thank you" every time someone mentioned his parents' death. Otherwise he acted so normal that soon everyone at school seemed to forget about it.

When the letter from Grandad finally arrived, Norah asked Aunt Florence to read it to them. She sat beside Gavin on the chesterfield, gripping his hand and crushing his fingers together.

Aunt Florence's voice was quiet and steady as she read:

Dear Norah and Gavin,

    I find it very difficult to tell you about Jane and Arthur's death, but it has to be done.

There isn't much to say about it. On Monday, March 12 your parents were having their noon meal at home. I was out at the pub when I heard the infernal ticking of a doodle-bug. We thought they were all over. There's a few seconds of quiet before the damned thing drops. When the explosion came so close we all rushed out of the pub and I ran home.

The house was smashed — just like my house in Camber was. So this is the second time I've escaped a Jerry bomb by being out. I want you to know I would gladly have gone in their place. It's so bloody unfair that an old man like me survived and they went.

They were killed instantly and would have felt no pain. Thank God you young ones weren't there as well. I never wanted you to go to Canada but since it probably saved your lives, I'm glad you went.

But now it's time for you to come back. The war's nearly over and you belong here. I know there still could be some danger, but everyone says that bomb was a fluke. We haven't seen any since and anyway, lightning never strikes twice in the same place. I am living with Muriel but I'm planning to rebuild the house. There's a lot that can be salvaged. I would like you both to live there with me. It's where you belong. Muriel and Barry and Tibby agree that would be best. We will all look after each other.

Regards to the Ogilvies. Please let me know immediately when you are coming back.

We can all stay with Muriel until the house is rebuilt.

Your affectionate grandfather,
James Loggin

A heavy silence filled the room. Gavin pretended to inspect Bosley's toenails. What did his guardians think of this rough-sounding man who said "damned" and "bloody"?

Aunt Florence spoke first. "Norah, dear, do you want to read the letter again alone?"

Norah took the piece of paper from her. Her face was almost as white as it was. "I'll read it again but we can talk now. How soon can we leave?"

"Norah!" gasped Aunt Mary.

Norah turned to her. "I'm sorry, Aunt Mary. I didn't mean to sound ungrateful. But we have to go home! Grandad needs us. And we can help him build the house again," she added, her voice breaking.

"Building the house isn't going to bring back your parents, Norah," said Aunt Mary gently.

"I know . . . but we have to go *home*," Norah pleaded. "Don't you understand?"

Aunt Florence had been unusually quiet. Now she patted Norah's knee and said in a strained voice, "Of course we understand. We've always known you would have to leave us. Now it's just more urgent. But *you* have to understand, Norah, how hard it's going to be for Mary and me. You're part of the family. We — we *love* you," she added stiffly.

Norah began to cry again. "I know that, Aunt

Florence. And we can't thank you enough for all you've done for us. But now it's time to go! *Isn't* it, Gavin . . ."

Gavin gulped and because Norah looked so desperate he nodded. "Uh-huh."

Aunt Florence glanced at him and then back at Norah. "Listen to me, Norah. I understand why you want to go back right away and why your grandfather wants you as soon as possible. Your family has had a terrible loss — you need to be with each other. But we can't just decide when you'll go. You heard what the social worker said. The ships are very erratic. If we tell them you want to go now it could be next week, or three weeks, or three months. None of us can live with that uncertainty."

"But —" protested Norah.

"Hear me out, please. I couldn't sleep nights if I thought we'd sent you back before the war's over. I don't agree with your grandfather about it being safe. What if there *are* more bombs in Kent? And it's important for you to finish your school year. You have final exams in June, which will help you get placed in an English school."

Aunt Florence sat up straighter, her voice growing more and more decided. "Here's my suggestion. Stay until the end of school. I'll tell the social service people we'd like to apply for a ship that sails *after* that — if the war's over by then, of course. You and Gavin have had a dreadful shock. I think you need time to recover before the additional change of returning to England. What do you think?

I'm sure your grandfather and sisters can wait a few more months," she finished grandly.

It took half an hour to convince Norah; half an hour in which Gavin sat in silent agony, praying she would agree. Finally she turned to him wearily. "What do *you* think, Gavin? Do you want to go back now or later?"

"Later, please," whispered Gavin. *Never*, he added to himself.

"All right. We'll wait until school's over." Norah sounded exhausted. She looked down at the letter in her hand and her face twitched.

"Come along, dear," said Aunt Mary. "I'm going to put you to bed with a hot drink and then I'll read to you."

Gavin twiddled the radio knobs after they'd left the room. He looked up to find Aunt Florence staring at him. Not with sorrow, which he would have expected, but with a kind of triumph. "What's wrong?" he asked.

"Nothing's wrong, pet," she smiled. She kissed the top of his head. "Nothing's wrong at all."

After that Norah acted more and more strangely. She alternated between profound sleepiness and bursts of anger. Hanny kept tempting her with her favourite food, but she scarcely ate. She yawned through meals and dozed on the chesterfield when they were all in the den.

"How is she ever going to get through her studies?" whispered Aunt Mary, as they looked at Norah curled up like a little girl in the cushions.

"I've written a note to her teacher to excuse her from homework for a week or so," said Aunt Florence. "He agrees with me that this is just a reaction to help her get over the shock."

Gavin tried to think up ways to make Norah feel better. He suggested they go to see *House of Frankenstein* but she refused. She never left the house except to go to school, and whenever Paige called on her she made up some excuse not to see her.

One afternoon Gavin was sent up to the tower to wake Norah for dinner. He sat on her bed while she got ready, chatting to her about school and normal things.

"How can you act as if nothing has happened?" she snapped.

She hadn't spoken to him like this since that long ago time when they'd first arrived.

"I'm sorry, Norah," whispered Gavin. "But I keep forgetting about it."

"Forgetting about it!" Norah glared at him. "How *could* you?"

"I guess . . . because . . . I don't feel as sad as you do. Because I don't remember Mum and Dad very well."

"*Try* to remember. It was only four and a half years ago that you saw them. *I* remember them perfectly! If only you remembered, we could talk about them. You're the only other person in this whole country who knew them!"

"I'm sorry, Norah. I'll try harder."

That night in bed he tried to envision his

parents' faces and voices: nothing. What was the matter with him? Roger hadn't seen his father since he was seven, and he often talked about things they had done together.

When Gavin tried to remember, a wall seemed to rise up between England and Canada. On one side was danger; on the other side, safety. The danger was worse than before: a bomb could smash a house and kill your relatives. That made the safety even more precious.

On Saturday Gavin borrowed his parents' letters and photographs from Norah. Surely if he studied these as intently as he studied for a social studies test it would *force* him to remember.

He began with the six photographs. The whole family before the war — Gavin smiled at Norah as a skinny little girl and himself as a solemn baby. Mum and Dad standing in front of "Little Whitebull," the house that was now demolished. Dad in his Home Guard uniform. Tibby in her A.T.S. uniform. Muriel and Barry holding their baby — Richard, the first grandchild. My nephew! thought Gavin. He'd forgotten about Richard. Mum and Dad and Grandad last summer.

His parents looked older than other people's parents. That was because there was such a gap between Norah and Gavin and their older sisters. Mum wore a kind of turban in all the pictures, so he couldn't tell what her hair was like. Her face was pretty but tired-looking. Dad's dark hair was streaked with grey. His beaky face was a lot like Norah's. Norah often told Gavin that *he* looked like

Mum, but he couldn't see the resemblance.

He would have recognized them if he saw them, because he'd had their faces pointed out in each new photograph as "Mum and Dad." But he recognized them the same way he did a picture of a famous actor or hockey star: someone familiar but not intimate.

Norah had kept all the letters in order, packed neatly into a wooden box Aunt Mary had given her. It took Gavin all day to read them. "What are you up to, all by yourself?" asked Aunt Florence when he went downstairs for a snack.

"Oh . . . just a special project." She smiled and didn't press further. That was one thing he'd always appreciated about Aunt Florence. Despite her constant shower of affection, she always respected his privacy.

The letters portrayed two people bravely struggling from day to day in war-torn England. Both his parents were extremely busy. Mum spent mornings at the Women's Voluntary Services and afternoons waiting in lines for food as rationing got worse. Dad worked all day as a bookkeeper in Gilden, the town near their village, and every evening at his Home Guard duties. But in between the hardships — and as he read Gavin sensed that there was a lot left out besides the sentences that had been blackened by the censor — his parents seemed to have had a lot of fun. There were dances that the American GIs put on in the village hall. Fetes to raise money, a community pig to feed. Marriages — including Muriel's — and other celebrations. Everyone in Ringden seemed to know each other and help each other get through the war.

Mum and Dad had taken turns to write. Every letter said how much they missed Norah and Gavin and looked forward to having them back.

They seemed like nice people to have as parents. He would have liked to know them. Now he never would. Now he was an *orphan* — like Oliver Twist. That felt important.

Reading the letters was like seeing a movie of the years he'd been in Canada. Each one commented on something Norah and Gavin had told their parents. "Congratulations on learning to swim, Gavin! . . . By the time you get this you will be back from your trip across Canada and enjoying Gairloch again . . . How exciting that you've begun skiing . . ."

Every time Gavin read words like this he remembered the thrill of learning to swim and ski, the exciting train journey west and every blissful summer at Gairloch. After he finished reading the letters he did have a clearer idea of what his parents had been like. But he was also left with a far stronger sense of what good years he'd enjoyed in Canada.

That evening he returned everything to Norah. "Did it help you remember them?" she asked, gazing sadly at the photographs.

"Not really," Gavin admitted. "But now I know them better." It was the best he could offer her.

The social worker came to see Norah and Gavin. She suggested that they both talk to a psychiatrist — "to sort out your feelings about this tragedy." One

afternoon they got to miss school while Aunt
Florence took them to the university on the streetcar.

Gavin felt strange when they walked past the
green space in front of an old stone building called
Hart House. He vaguely remembered playing
games on this grass the week they had stayed at the
university until they'd gone to live with the
Ogilvies. It seemed like centuries ago.

They entered another old building. Gavin sat
with Aunt Florence in a waiting room while Norah
was led into an office and a door closed. Gavin
swung his legs and tried to read a babyish children's
book that was on a table. Aunt Florence stared into
space, unusually vague.

After a long time Norah came out, looking
angry and proud. Then it was Gavin's turn. A
woman with a chirpy, brisk voice invited him to sit
down on a slippery chair in front of her desk.

Aunt Florence had told him that a psychiatrist
was like a doctor who took care of your feelings
instead of your body. "In my day we didn't need to
talk to strangers about our personal affairs," she
sniffed. "But they seem to think it will be helpful."

The woman — she told Gavin to call her Dr
Wilson — started by asking him to tell her about
the things he did every day. He wondered why she
was so interested, but he chatted to her about his
friends and Bosley and Cubs. Every time he
sounded enthusiastic about something, like getting
a home run or enjoying a book, she smiled and said
"Good for you." So he was careful not to tell her
anything that would make her stop smiling —

nothing unpleasant or confusing about Mick, or Eleanor.

At last she came to the subject of his parents. "Do you feel sad about what happened?" she asked kindly.

Gavin squirmed. He couldn't tell her he didn't — then she wouldn't think he was a good person. He nodded, trying to look doleful.

"How much do you remember about them?"

Gavin swallowed hard. "Well, of *course* I remember them — but not as much as Norah does."

"It would be very natural if you didn't remember much," she said. "Or if you don't feel *very* sad. After all, you were only five the last time you saw them."

She smiled and Gavin gave her a timid smile in return. So he didn't have to remember — that was a relief. He would have liked to tell her how much he *wanted* to remember, for Norah's sake. But he thought of Aunt Florence's words. This woman was a stranger; he didn't know her at all.

"And how do you feel about going back to England?"

Gavin thought fast, so she wouldn't find out what a coward he was. "I'm sad about leaving the Ogilvies of course, but I'm *English*," he explained, remembering Norah's words. "That's where I belong."

She seemed to believe him. "Good for you!" she repeated. She sighed. "It's going to be much harder for your sister. Being home will bring back so many sad memories for her."

She stood up. "*You* seem to be coping very well,

Gavin. You're a brave little boy, and I've enjoyed talking to you." She shook his hand and walked him to the door. Then Aunt Florence went in.

"She was so nosy!" said Gavin. "What did she say to you, Norah?"

"Oh . . . nothing worth mentioning." Norah buried her nose in a *National Geographic* magazine. Gavin left her alone. Finally Aunt Florence came out and they all went home.

"Dr Wilson says that Norah's reactions are completely normal," Aunt Florence told Aunt Mary that evening when Norah was upstairs. "We just have to wait. She assures me she'll get over it with time."

"The poor dear," sighed Aunt Mary.

Aunt Florence smiled at Gavin. "And she says you're doing fine, pet."

Gavin felt as if he'd passed some sort of test — a test he'd cheated on.

VII

The Dog Show

Easter passed very quietly in the Ogilvie household. Usually they went to the Royal York Hotel for Sunday dinner after church, followed by a walk on the boardwalk at Sunnyside. But this year they just came home and had a small ham. Gavin munched on it gloomily. He didn't like ham, but he couldn't complain when it was so hard to get.

Today was April Fools' Day as well as Easter. But this year he couldn't subsitute salt for sugar at breakfast, or tell people things like "There's a spider in your hair" or "Your shoe lace is undone." The family was still too sad for jokes. Since April the first was on a Sunday he couldn't even enjoy the tricks they always played in school. And now it was past noon and April Fools' was over anyway.

Norah had refused to go to church. "I don't

believe in God any more," she told the aunts bluntly.

"But Norah!" cried Aunt Mary. "It's understandable that you would feel that way, but when something terrible happens you *need* to go to church!"

"Well, I'm not," said Norah. "I'm never going again and you can't make me."

Aunt Florence opened her mouth to scold Norah, then closed it and gave her a disapproving look instead.

Gavin was awed by Norah's nerve. But she was right, he thought. They couldn't make her go to church. Aunt Mary offered to make an appointment for her to talk to Reverend Milne, but Norah firmly refused.

A few days later Paige persuaded Norah to go over to her house. But Norah was back in twenty minutes. "She says I sat down on her favourite record on purpose," she told Gavin. "How was *I* supposed to know it was on the chair? What a stupid place to leave a record! I'm not speaking to Paige any more." She ran upstairs.

Then Norah's teacher asked Aunt Florence for a conference. "He says you're being rude in class," Aunt Florence told her. "He's trying to be as understanding as he can, but you are really testing his patience, Norah. We all know you're grieving for your parents, but you must try to co-operate."

"Why should I?" snapped Norah. "Who cares? I'll soon be finished with this crummy school anyway." Again, she fled to her tower.

"I don't see why she should get away with this rudeness," snorted Aunt Florence.

"But Mother," objected Aunt Mary, "didn't Dr Wilson say it's healthy for her to be angry?"

Aunt Florence sighed. "I suppose so. If Norah were really my child I'd insist on her being polite to her elders. But I guess we'll just have to put up with it."

Gavin wished he hadn't overheard this. Aunt Florence had always treated Gavin and Norah as if they *were* her children. Now she seemed to be letting Norah go.

Was she letting him go too? Was that why she wasn't making more of a fuss about him leaving in a few months? But maybe she just wanted to ignore that as much as he was.

Gavin tried to enjoy the unusually early spring as if it were like any other April. After he saw the movie *Thunderhead, Son of Flicka* he named his bicycle Thunderhead and rode it along the road like a real stallion. The gardens in Rosedale blazed with yellow forsythia and by the third week in April the new green leaves had already popped open.

At school, Mick had suddenly stopped bullying. He began combing his hair and tucking in his shirt. Everyone was relieved, but puzzled. Then Roger found out why.

"You know Terry Fraser, who's in the chess club with me?" Tim and Gavin nodded. "Well, he told me Mick's in love with his sister Doris!"

"Mick? In *love*?" giggled Tim.

Roger grinned. "Yes! He keeps asking her for dates but she won't go. He follows her home every day and writes her notes. Doris just laughs at them. She showed them to Terry — he says they're really corny."

"Poor Doris!" said Tim.

"At least it keeps him busy," said Gavin. Now they didn't have to keep out of Mick's way. But every once in a while Mick would give Gavin that strange look — as if he wanted something from him.

Aunt Mary took Gavin with her on the train to visit an old friend in St Catharines. She was in rhapsody over the cherry blossoms but Gavin was more interested in Niagara Falls, where the friend, Mrs Butler, drove them. He had been there several times before, but he always found the falls a thrill.

He stared in wonder at the powerful roar of water, his face soaked with spray. The biggest waterfall in the world. It just kept going — thundering endlessly over the rocks, oblivious of tourists or wars or ten-year-old boys. Somehow its indifference was comforting.

Gavin turned around to the two women. "The Canadian falls are *much* bigger than the American falls."

"Listen to him!" chuckled Mrs Butler. "He sounds like a real Canadian!"

Gavin was offended. Of course he was a Canadian! Then he remembered that he wasn't.

The grown-ups' lives revolved around the news. President Roosevelt had died. War brides began to arrive in Canada. The world held its breath with excitement as it waited for the final defeat. Everyone began guessing the exact date when the war would end.

Tim showed Gavin and Roger a clipping from the paper. A Junior Dog Show was to be held at Poplar Park that Saturday. "Why don't we enter Bosley?" said Tim. "The first prize is a book of movie tickets!"

Gavin studied the announcement. There were six categories Bosley could enter: Most Obedient, Waggiest Tail, Best Costume, Best Groomed, Funniest Expression and Best in Show.

Every day that week he brushed Bosley until his coat gleamed like black-and-white satin. He found one of his outgrown Hallowe'en costumes for Bosley to wear: a clown suit trimmed with orange and green ruffles. He cut holes in the orange wig for Bosley's ears.

Bosley had always been obedient. Gavin practised his "wave," "trust and paid for" and "play dead" tricks. He worked out a routine where the dog jumped over a box to fetch a ball, then came back with it to perch on the box. "You're such a *good* dog," Gavin whispered to him the night before the show. "You're just as clever as Lassie. I know you'll win everything."

Bosley bounded beside the three boys on the way to Poplar Park. Gavin carried the box and the others the ball and costume.

As they approached they could hear barking and yelling. Kids and dogs were everywhere. A small girl tried to keep up with an excited

Newfoundland dragging her on its leash. Three golden retrievers panted at their owners' feet, grinning at everyone. A tiny papillon huddled inside its owner's jacket.

"Please control your dogs!" shouted one of the adults in charge, as a pug and a curly-haired mutt tumbled in a fight around her feet.

Bosley took one look at the noisy crowd and pressed against Gavin's knee. A cairn terrier snapped at his feet. Bosley whimpered and put his tail between his legs. Daphne Worsley ran up and picked up the terrier's leash.

"It's all right, Boz," said Gavin, as Bosley tried to hide behind him. "It's only Thistle. You *know* Thistle!"

"Bosley's such a coward," said Daphne smugly. "He's always been afraid of my dog."

"He is not a coward!" said Gavin.

"He's going to win everything — just wait," said Roger.

Daphne picked up Thistle. "Huh! Just *you* wait. Thistle'll win way more ribbons than Bosley."

Gavin turned his back on her and tried to calm Bosley, as a man with a megaphone announced the first category: The Dog with the Waggiest Tail. Bosley kept his tail firmly planted between his legs.

"Come on, Boz — want a biscuit?" Gavin cried desperately. He always wagged his tail for a biscuit — but not today. Tim tried to hold up the spaniel's tail but when he let it go the tail snapped back out of sight.

"Do something!" said Roger. "They're all in the ring!"

"I can't," sighed Gavin. "He'll just have to skip this category." They watched with disgust as Thistle, his tail straight up and whipping back and forth like a metronome, won first prize.

Next was Obedience. "He'll win this," said Gavin confidently. He pulled Bosley into the ring. The dog reluctantly rolled over and played dead, trembling the whole time. When Gavin ordered "Trust" he obediently sat and ignored the biscuit in front of him; but at "Paid For" he wouldn't touch it, despite Gavin's pleading. He half-heartedly jumped over the box to retrieve the ball, but it landed beside Thistle. The terrier growled and Bosley raced back to Gavin without the ball, yelping with fright while the audience laughed.

"What's *wrong* with him?" asked Tim.

"He's just not used to being here yet," said Gavin. "He'll improve." They watched Daphne and her dog prance into the ring. "Thistle will be worse than Bosley," whispered Gavin. "He *never* obeys."

But Daphne had worked out a routine involving the one thing Thistle was excellent at: jumping. She arranged three boxes in a row and Thistle bounced back and forth over them like a dog on springs, yipping proudly. The audience loved it and the terrier won another First.

They watched Toby the papillon and Amos the Newfoundland win for smallest and largest dog. Then they decked Bosley out in his clown outfit and paraded him around the ring for Best Costume.

Bosley dragged his feet and Gavin had to pull him. Then he sat down and pawed off his wig. Ahead of them strutted Thistle, wearing a tiny kilt tied around his middle and a Scottish beret with holes cut out for his ears. Daphne wore a matching kilt and hat.

"First prize for Thistle again!" groaned Tim when the event was over.

"It's not fair," said Gavin. "The rules didn't say anything about the *owners* dressing up."

"We'll never get Best in Show now," said Roger sadly. "There go the movie tickets."

But then Bosley improved. He was third for Best Groomed and first for Funniest Expression. "To Bosley, the springer spaniel, because he looks so dejected about being here," said the judge.

"Just ignore them, Boz," whispered Gavin as everyone laughed again. "At least you won."

He and Tim and Roger watched as Daphne took Thistle up to receive the ribbon for Best in Show — and the book of tickets.

"Don't worry, Boz," said Gavin. "*I* know you're the best dog in the world!"

Bosley whined at him pleadingly, as if he were saying "Can't we go home now?"

"We'll go soon," promised Gavin. "First we're getting popcorn and you can have some."

Eleanor was standing beside the popcorn stand. Her monkey sat on her shoulder, playing with one of her braids. "Hi," she called.

"Can I hold Kilroy?" asked Tim.

"Better not," she said calmly. "He bites strangers. I tried to enter him in the show but they said only dogs were eligible. It's so unfair! Kilroy is as good as any dog."

The monkey was dressed in a green suit, like a little man. He even wore a tie. He bared his teeth and chittered at Bosley and Bosley got as far away from him as he could.

"He's a swell monkey," said Gavin. He smiled at Eleanor while Tim and Roger were buying their popcorn. She smiled back. "Your dog's nice too," she said.

Eleanor's sister led her away and the boys sat on the grass, wolfing down popcorn. Bosley wouldn't eat and still gave Gavin beseeching looks, but Gavin didn't want to go home yet. The Ogilvies' house was so dismal and boring these days, with Norah wretched and Aunt Florence and Aunt Mary wrapped up in the news.

Today was the first day since Gavin's parents' death when no one had come up to him to mention it. The sun was out, the duck pond sparkled in the bright air, and dogs panted and played around him. Bosley hadn't done very well, but it didn't matter. Nobody in the crowd around him would ever guess that Gavin wasn't a Canadian boy and that Bosley didn't really belong to him.

VIII

The Lights Go On

"Have you heard?" shouted Tim before he reached Gavin. "Hitler's dead!"

"I know!" said Gavin. Hanny had burnt the toast at breakfast while Aunt Florence read aloud the newspaper. Mussolini was dead too. There was a photograph of his body in the same paper.

Adolph Hitler . . . the evil man they had been fighting against as long as Gavin could remember. When he'd first come to Canada he'd had nightmares about Hitler, but after he started school he had made fun of him like everyone else: a silly little man with a stubby moustache. But one of Hitler's bombs had killed his parents . . .

"Aren't you glad?" said Tim, while they waited for Roger.

"Of course!" said Gavin. But the paper had also said that a German surrender was "imminent."

That meant the war could be over this week —
so he and Norah would have to go back to England
as soon as the school year finished.

"My Mum bought me a flag for VE Day," said
Roger after he'd joined them.

"We should get some bunting and decorate our
bikes so we'll be ready," said Tim.

Mrs Moss spent half of arithmetic talking about
the news. "You are a privileged generation," she
told them. "You'll inherit a world of peace that your
elders won for you."

The class grew more and more restless as
they thought of victory — and a holiday from
school. "What if it happens on the *weekend*?"
worried Roger.

The next day Berlin fell. Norah stopped Gavin
on the stairs. "We can go home soon," she said
quietly.

"Uh-huh," gulped Gavin.

"I finally had a letter from Andrew," said
Norah. "Now he's in Holland. He says he'll visit us
in England if we're there before he comes back to
Canada."

"How is he?"

"He always *says* he's fine. It's hard to tell how
he really is. I bet he isn't fine. I bet he's hated it,
having to kill people. But at least *he* wasn't killed,"
she added bitterly. "He said to tell you how sorry he
is about Mum and Dad."

"Mmm," said Gavin. He tried to imagine
Andrew visiting them in England but he couldn't
even picture himself there.

And what would happen with Andrew and Norah? He couldn't tell from his sister's voice whether she still loved Andrew.

Everything was happening much too fast, like the last of the water rushing out of a tub. Gavin wanted to put in the plug. At the same time, he couldn't help being infected by the joy of victory that was sweeping the city.

Next Monday morning Gavin stood outside Mr Evans's office with the other messengers for that week. When you were a messenger you waited there every day to take news back to the classroom.

The principal was usually a vague, subdued man. But this morning he actually ran out of his office, a smile creasing his tired-looking face.

A few seconds later Gavin skidded along the wooden floor back to his classroom. He pushed open the door and cried, "The war's over! Mr Evans just told us! He wants to see you right away, Mrs Moss."

Class 5A leapt to their feet, pounded on their desks and cheered. Mrs Moss didn't even try to stop them. She ran out of the room and returned quickly.

Then she asked them to sit down. Everyone became quiet when they noticed her wet eyes. Cheers and thumps were still coming from other classrooms down the corridor.

"The war in Europe is indeed over," said Mrs Moss. "The Germans surrendered last night. I think it's especially appropriate that you were the one to tell us, Gavin, when your family and country have

suffered so much." She beamed at them. "Now . . .
Mr Evans has informed me that today *and* tomorrow
will be a holiday . . ."

"Hooray!" Pandemonium broke out again, but
Mrs Moss waved it down. "*Quiet*, please . . . that's
better. I know you're eager to go out and celebrate,
but before we go we'll have a short service of
thanksgiving."

She read aloud a prayer about peace, then they
sang "The Maple Leaf Forever."

"All right," she smiled. "Off you go."

Gavin, Roger and Tim galloped home, leaping
into the air and shouting. The sidewalks teemed
with released children.

"Okay," panted Tim at the corner. "Get your
bikes and meet here in fifteen minutes. Then we'll
go downtown!"

Gavin kept running. His heart pounded so
much he had to stop and catch his breath before he
dashed up the steps and pushed open the door.

"Aunt Florence! Aunt Mary! Hanny! The war's
over!" He forgot that he had wished it would never
end.

They all came out of the den. "We know, pet,"
said Aunt Florence, hugging him. "We've just been
listening to Mr Churchill."

"School's closed!" said Gavin. "Can I go downtown on my bike with Tim and Roger?"

Aunt Florence smiled. "I suppose so, if you're
careful. Hanny, why don't you go home and celebrate with your husband? Mary and I will stay here
and listen to the news."

"Thank you, Mrs Ogilvie," said Hanny. "I'll just pack Gavin a sandwich before I go."

"I'm going to put up that old Union Jack that's in the attic!" said Aunt Mary. Her face looked as excited as a girl's.

Norah walked slowly into the hall, dropping her books. "The war's over. I guess you already know," she added in a dull voice.

Aunt Mary kissed her. "Yes, dear Norah. This long, terrible war is finally over. Are you going to go downtown and celebrate, like Gavin?"

"Celebrate? Why would I want to celebrate?"

Gavin left the aunts trying to comfort her.

The three boys rode to the corner of Bay and Queen, then hid their bicycles under the stairs of a building and joined the noisy crowd around City Hall. A tall red thermometer decorated its clock tower, keeping track of the Victory Bond Drive.

Above them people threw ticker tape from high office windows and Mosquito aircraft dropped bags of paper scraps, until the air looked like December's snowstorm. Music blared from loudspeakers and the Mayor stepped onto a platform and led the crowd in singing "God Save the King."

Gavin and Tim and Roger pushed their way through the swaying, cheering crowd. Adults ruffled their hair or pulled them into impromptu dances. They caught sight of other kids from their school and waved. Then they spotted some boys hitching a ride on the front of a streetcar.

"Come on," shouted Tim. When the next streetcar arrived they perched in a row on its front fender for a few minutes, then hopped off — right in front of a policeman. But he just grinned at them.

They stayed downtown until their throats were sore from shouting and singing, their legs ached from standing and their stomachs rumbled. As they pushed their way back to their bikes, Gavin noticed a soldier standing on the sidewalk. He was watching everyone quietly, his sombre expression a contrast to the giddy crowd. One khaki sleeve was pinned up neatly where the soldier's arm was missing.

When he got home Gavin told the aunts and Norah all about the downtown celebrations. "May I go out again after dinner?" he asked. "They're having fireworks in Poplar Park!"

"Norah's going to watch them," smiled Aunt Mary. "Paige phoned and asked her. Aren't you, Norah dear . . ."

Norah looked indifferent. "I guess so. Gavin can come with us if he wants."

Aunt Florence shook her head. "I think you've had enough excitement, pet. And I've hardly seen you all day! You can watch the fireworks from here."

"But how?"

She smiled mysteriously. "You'll see. You'll have a better view than anyone in Toronto!"

When Paige called for Norah she looked as if she wanted to change her mind about going out. But Paige dragged her away before she could refuse.

Then Aunt Florence led Aunt Mary and Gavin

up the back stairs to the former maid's room. Gavin stared at it curiously. When he'd first come here there had been a sulky live-in maid called Edith. But Edith had left to work in an airplane factory and Aunt Florence had never found a replacement.

Now Aunt Florence stood on a chair and pushed open a trap door in the roof. A ladder swung down. She laughed at Gavin's surprised face. "Come on, pet — you'll have to go first and help us up."

Gavin scurried up the ladder and stepped onto — the top of the house! There was a flat roof area covered with a thin layer of gravel. He leaned back into the cavity and pulled up the chairs they handed him. Then he gave a hand to Aunt Mary and together they heaved up the bulk of Aunt Florence.

"I didn't know you could come up here!" said Gavin. "Why didn't you tell me?"

Aunt Florence chuckled. "Because I didn't want you — or your unruly sister — to come up on your own. You're never to do that, do you understand? It's a very long way down."

Gavin nodded reluctantly. He explored the whole of the roof while his guardians set up the chairs. Then the three of them sat in a row and looked down at the lit-up city.

The Ogilvies' house was one of the tallest in the neighbourhood. A sea of black roofs and green tree-tops was spread out below them in the dusk. Gavin could see the Worsleys' yard, where Thistle raced around yapping. Daphne came out and called him and Gavin smiled to himself. She didn't know she was being watched.

"Hugh and I sometimes came up here," said Aunt Mary. "On the maid's day off."

"What?" Aunt Florence stared at her daughter. "I didn't know you even knew about it!"

"Hugh found the door when he was twelve and I was nine. We came up for years. Once even at night!"

"Mary! I simply cannot believe you would do such a thing!" spluttered Aunt Florence — as if Aunt Mary were *still* nine.

"Well, we did."

Aunt Mary smiled calmly at her mother and, very slowly, Aunt Florence smiled back. "I guess I can't do anything about it now. That Hugh . . ." she added sadly, gazing at Gavin in the hungry way she always did when she mentioned her son.

"The fireworks are starting!" said Gavin. A silvery fountain burst in the distance, then a blue streak and a pink star. The screeches and crackles reached them a little later than the flashes, like a movie where the sound didn't match the picture. After the fireworks they could hear sirens, ringing church bells and faint, distant singing.

"The lights will be blazing in England tonight," said Aunt Florence. "Your grandfather and sisters will be glad of that, Gavin."

"The European war over at last," sighed Aunt Mary. "Now if they can just finish the war with Japan as well, maybe that will be an end to this madness. It's hard to feel happy when it's brought so much tragedy. Especially to you and Norah, Gavin." She pounded the arm of her chair. "Oh, *when* will people ever learn that war doesn't solve anything?"

The other two stared at this unusual outburst. "Now, Mary . . . let's count our blessings," said Aunt Florence. "We got rid of that brutish Hitler. Gavin and Norah were free from danger in Canada. Andrew is safe. And Gavin was too young to be in it. Let's hope you'll *never* have to be in a war, sweetness." She patted his knee. Gavin was once again surprised that she was not saying anything about him going back to England.

He looked up at both of them: ridiculous, loving Aunt Florence, and good Aunt Mary. These two women were his parents now. He got up and pretended to look at some revellers coming home from the fireworks, but he was blinking back tears. How could he leave them?

The next day — the *official* VE Day — Gavin and Tim and Roger went downtown again but it was quieter than the day before. They bicycled to Queen Street and watched a parade, then went to Tim's house for lunch.

"I want to show you something," Tim told them, after his mother had gone out with his younger brothers. He led Gavin and Roger to his parents' room and pulled out a magazine from under the mattress.

"I heard Mum tell Dad she was going to hide this from us," said Tim. "So I sneaked in and found it."

Gavin recognized the cover. "Why would your parents hide *Life*?"

"This issue is so creepy, I guess they thought it would scare us. It is scary. Are you brave enough to look?"

Of course the other two had to say they were. They knelt on the floor and leaned on the bed while Tim opened the magazine. Then they stared in silence, while he slowly turned the pages.

The full-page photographs were of bodies. Terrible, emaciated, naked bodies. *Hundreds* of bodies. In one picture they were being shovelled into a mass grave.

Gavin swallowed. "But — but who are they?" he croaked.

"It says they're in some camps in Germany called Belsen and Buchenwald," said Tim, sounding out the names with difficulty. "But it doesn't say who they are or why they're dead. Or why there's so many of them."

Gavin turned back the pages and read some of the text. "It says they're 'slave labourers.' What does that mean?"

"I didn't know the Germans had slaves," said Tim. "Do you think they were Allies?"

"We could ask a grown-up," said Roger.

"But then they'd find out we were looking at this when we weren't supposed to," said Tim.

They continued to stare at the hideous pages. Gavin shivered. "Let's put it away. Maybe one day we'll find out who they are."

Tim shoved the magazine under the mattress and they went out to play in the sunshine.

IX

A Proposal

"Gavin, I'd like to talk to you in my room," said Aunt Florence the next evening.

Gavin finished putting on his pyjamas and went in to sit on the soft loveseat in her bedroom. Aunt Florence sank down beside him. "You may have noticed," she began, "that I've been out a lot lately."

Now that he thought of it, she had gone downtown for many "appointments" in the past few weeks. But Aunt Florence was often out, visiting friends or meeting with one of her charity groups.

"I've been working out a plan, Gavin, and now I need your advice. It's an idea that came to me as soon as we heard about your parents. It wouldn't have been appropriate to bring it up then. But now it's time, especially since the war's over."

"What is it?"

"I know that Norah has to return to England," said Aunt Florence slowly. "She's never felt totally at home in Canada, although she's adjusted as well as she could. It's understandable that she wants to go back. She was old enough when she left to remember her own country."

She paused. "But you're different, Gavin. You feel like a Canadian now — am I right?"

Gavin nodded. What was she getting at?

"And I think you're happy living with Mary and me." Her eyes gleamed, knowing the answer.

"Of course!"

"I know you are," she said warmly. "From the moment you came here you belonged — much more than Norah did. Now, Gavin, I'm going to ask you something that will startle you. You don't have to answer right away." She put both her hands on his shoulders and looked into his eyes. "Would you like to stay in Canada and live with me always?"

Gavin started to shiver, the joy that filled him was so intense. "Stay in Canada? But how?"

"You've been like a son to me these past years. Now I'd like you to be my *real* son. I want to adopt you, Gavin. I would never have suggested this, of course, when your parents were alive. I knew it was going to be difficult for you to return, but they were your parents — you belonged with them. But now that they've gone, you can stay here! If you'd like to, of course."

Gavin took a deep breath. "Could you adopt Bosley too?"

Aunt Florence threw back her head and laughed. "Of course I'll adopt Bosley, you funny boy! I know Reg would give him to you for good. Everything would be the same. You and Bosley would keep on living here with Mary and me and you'd become a real Canadian."

"But what about *Norah*?"

"That's the hard part, pet," said Aunt Florence gently. "You and Norah would be separated. I know how much you love your sister. But she's growing up. She'll be leaving you one day anyway. We would certainly have her back to Canada whenever she wanted to come. And we could visit her often in England."

"But why can't you adopt Norah too?"

Aunt Florence sighed. "I would. I really would, Gavin, despite our differences, but you know she wouldn't want it. She wants to return to England and I don't blame her."

Gavin thought of something else. "Will my grandfather *let* you adopt me?"

"You've hit upon the one problem we might have. No, he might not let me, and if he objects I won't be able to — he's your legal guardian now." A familiar stubborn expression appeared on her face. "But I think I can persuade him — him and your older sisters and maybe even Norah. I'll see that you get a good education. In grade seven you can start St Martin's, which is the best boys' school in Ontario. And then university. And you could take piano lessons and French lessons — you'll have every advantage. And, most important — you would become my heir."

"Your air?" said Gavin. "What does that mean?"

"It means that one day — along with Mary, of course — you'll inherit this," smiled Aunt Florence, waving her hand around her. "Surely your family wouldn't want to deny you *that*."

She leaned over and kissed him. "I know this is a lot for you to take in, pet. I don't want you to give me an answer yet. Think about it until the weekend, all right?"

"But can't I tell Norah?"

"If you want. But I don't think you should tell her until you're sure of your decision. You know she'll be against it. Why wouldn't she? And this is a secret, all right? I've told Mary, but I don't think you should discuss it with anyone else but Norah."

Gavin could hardly make it into bed, he was so stunned. He put down one arm and fondled Bosley, grinning into the darkness.

He didn't need any time to think about it. He had never wanted anything as much in his life. If Aunt Florence adopted him everything would stay the same! He could keep Bosley! He would be safe and secure in Canada instead of living in a scary country where people had been killed by bombs. There would be no Norah, but as wave after wave of relief swept over Gavin he tried not to think about that.

For the rest of the week Gavin thought he would burst with the excitement of Aunt Florence's proposal. "We'll be able to keep going to Gairloch every summer, Boz," he whispered to the dog. "We'll always know Tim and Roger. Next year you can go in the Dog Show again, and this time you'll win!"

He didn't think he wanted to go to a posh boys' school and wear a uniform, but that was two years away. Maybe by then he could talk Aunt Florence out of it.

The future, which had been a black tunnel, now seemed like a long vista of sunny days. Gavin walked around holding a bubble of happiness inside him. Every time he looked at Aunt Florence or Aunt Mary they exchanged secretive smiles. He knew that Aunt Florence guessed what he'd decided, but he'd promised to wait until the weekend to tell her.

And he *should* talk to Norah before then. But every time he began to climb the stairs to her room he thought of a reason to wait until later. In the daytime it was easy to revel in the joy of staying in Canada. But at night he twisted in his sheets, thinking about Norah.

If only she could stay too! But he knew she wouldn't, not even for him. He tried to reassure himself with what Aunt Florence had said — that Norah would be leaving him anyway. She was getting as grown-up as his other sisters. One day she might get married, like Muriel, or get a job, like Tibby.

But Norah was the only sister he knew. She was his best friend. How could he face those clear eyes and tell her he was staying behind?

He could picture exactly how she'd react. They

were so different from each other. Norah always knew what she wanted. She was so sure about everything, so brave. He was so wishy-washy . . . such a coward.

He couldn't tell her.

"I've decided," he announced to Aunt Florence on Saturday morning. "I'll stay. I'll stay and be your son."

"Oh, Gavin." Aunt Florence clasped him so hard that Gavin couldn't breathe. "Let go!" he laughed.

She loosened her hold. There were tears in her eyes. "You have made me very, very happy. And I'll make *you* happy, you'll see. You'll be the happiest boy in Canada!" she crowed, kissing him firmly on each cheek.

"There's still Norah and Grandad," Gavin reminded her.

"Did you talk to Norah?"

Gavin hung his head. "I couldn't," he whispered. "Could *you* tell her?"

For a second a flicker of fear passed over Aunt Florence's face. Then she straightened her blouse and said briskly. "All right, pet. Why don't you send her down to me right now? We might as well get this over with."

"What does *she* want?" demanded Norah, when Gavin appeared at her door. "I'm trying to finish my essay."

"Just go and see her," said Gavin. He put his hand on Norah's arm as she brushed past him. "And Norah . . . *listen* to her, okay?"

Norah gave him a quizzical look and flounced downstairs. Gavin followed slowly. His mouth was dry and his stomach churned. He sat on the floor outside his room and watched Aunt Florence's closed door. Bosley's warm side pressed against him.

At first he heard the low, reasoned murmur of Aunt Florence's words. Norah's response was swift and sure: "*No!*" Gavin clutched Bosley as her voice grew louder. "He's not staying! You can't *do* this!"

"What's going on?" Aunt Mary had come out of her room.

Gavin gave her a desperate look. "Aunt Florence is telling Norah."

"The poor child," murmured Aunt Mary. "I wonder if this idea of Mother's is right . . ."

Gavin couldn't bear to be left out any longer. He stood up and opened the door. Norah and Aunt Florence were facing each other like two opponents in a boxing ring. Both pairs of grey eyes flashed with determination. Norah looked much angrier, however, while Aunt Florence was struggling to stay calm.

"I knew you'd react this way, Norah," she said. "But I think that once you've thought about it, you'll see it's the best thing for Gavin. Isn't he the one we should be thinking about?"

"Gavin is not staying in Canada!" shouted Norah.

Desperation filled Gavin. Norah was standing in his way — destroying his only chance of safety and happiness.

"Listen to me, Norah!" They all stared at him with surprise. "I *want* to stay! I *want* to live in Canada!" Her hurt expression melted his anger into tears. "Oh, Norah . . . why can't you stay too?"

"I have already suggested to Norah that I adopt her as well," said Aunt Florence stiffly. "She says she would rather go back to England."

"But *I* want to stay here!" begged Gavin. "*Please*, Norah . . ."

Norah looked around at all of them. Her face was bleached of colour and her voice icy. "All right, Gavin — stay. You can have him, Aunt Florence. And you can all just — go — to — hell!" She spun around and ran out of the room.

By the evening they were limp from spent emotion. Aunt Florence had gone up to Norah's room and stayed there a long time.

"She wants to speak to you now," she told Gavin. She shut herself up with Aunt Mary and Gavin trudged up the stairs to the tower.

"Come in," said Norah weakly. She was lying on her bed. "Listen, Gavin," she muttered. "I'm sorry I said that awful thing. I didn't mean it. Do you believe me?"

"Yes," whispered Gavin, although he didn't think he'd ever forget the sting of those words. Words *hurt*. He sat down on the end of the bed, keeping as far away from Norah as he could. Her voice still sounded bitter and she looked as terrible as when they'd heard about their parents. Her hair was in uncombed strings over her tear-marked cheeks and her nose was raw from crying. *He* had made her feel this way.

"Do you really want to stay here?" Norah asked him.

Gavin nodded miserably. He was wounding her even more but he had no choice.

"Are you sure Aunt Florence hasn't just brainwashed you into saying yes? She's always had some sort of weird power over you."

"I made up my own mind. I'm sorry, Norah. I *have* to stay, don't you see? Canada's my *home*. I don't *remember* England. I don't even remember —" He stopped, afraid to hurt her again.

"You don't remember Mum and Dad," she sighed. "I know that now."

"I don't want to lose *you*," said Gavin. "But Aunt Florence said we can visit you, and you can visit us too."

"She told me that too." Norah sat up. "Aunt Florence is offering you a lot," she said tightly. "You'll get a good education and one day you'll be rich."

And I'll get to keep Bosley, Gavin added to himself.

"She seems to think it's the best thing for you," continued Norah. "I don't! But Aunt Florence always gets what she wants. I just hope Grandad refuses — I bet he will."

She finally managed a small, clenched smile. "But I also want you to be happy, Gavin. Aunt Florence says I shouldn't upset you about it. So I'll keep quiet until we hear Grandad's decision. That's the best I can offer."

"Thank you," whispered Gavin. He had to leave before he cried. He ran down to his room and crawled under his eiderdown.

What a horrible, horrible day. It was even worse than when his parents died, because this time all the anguish revolved around *him*. He gazed around his neat room, at his models and soldiers and books arranged exactly as he liked them. In Muriel's house in England he probably wouldn't even have his own room.

Surely Grandad would say yes and Norah would accept it. Then maybe he could stop feeling so guilty.

Aunt Florence sent Grandad a cable, asking him to telephone at her expense. To Norah's fury, the call came through when they were in school. "I wanted to talk to him!" she cried.

"He's going to phone back again," said Aunt Florence. "Maybe you can talk to him then. His voice was amazingly clear."

"But what did he *say*?" demanded Norah.

She looked embarrassed. "He was . . . well . . . surprised, of course. He said he'd think about my proposal and phone back. I did most of the talking."

"I bet you did," Norah muttered, so low that only Gavin heard her.

Then a cable arrived:

MUST CONSULT REST FAMILY STOP WILL
NOT TELEPHONE UNTIL JUNE
JAMES LOGGIN

"June!" spluttered Aunt Florence. "That's too long! Doesn't he realize how hard it is on Gavin to wait? And we can't make any arrangements for a ship until we know if one or both of you are going."

"But Mother," said Aunt Mary timidly, "you can understand how Mr Loggin needs time to think about it. After all, you're asking him to give up his only grandson." Aunt Florence frowned at her.

Gavin stole a glance at Norah. She looked as frustrated as the rest of them not to *know*.

"Well, he's left us no choice," sighed Aunt Florence. Later she told Gavin in private not to worry. "He didn't sound negative, pet — just rather shocked, which is understandable. Let's assume you *are* staying. I'm going to write a long letter to your grandfather. I'm sure I can convince him. But until we know, remember it's still a secret."

But Gavin couldn't keep the secret bottled up any longer. One afternoon, when he and Tim and Roger were in the fort, he told his friends that he might stay in Canada.

"Hooray!" shouted Tim. Roger just grinned.

"Don't tell anyone," warned Gavin. "It's a secret! And my grandfather might *make* me go back."

"He must be really mean to do that," said Roger.

This was exactly how Gavin had been imagining Grandad lately — a mean old man who wanted to spoil his happiness.

"He *is* mean," said Gavin. "It would be awful to have to live with him. We don't even have a house! We'd have to squeeze into my sister's house.

And she and her husband are probably mean too,"
he added wildly. He looked at their sympathetic
faces. "But wouldn't it be keen if I stayed in Canada?
Then we'd always be friends!"

"I have an idea," said Tim. "Let's make a pact,
just in case you do have to go back. A pact in blood."

"Blood!" the other two cried.

"Just a little bit of blood," said Tim. "We'll prick
our fingers and be blood brothers, the way they did
in *Secret Water*." They were all avid readers of the
Arthur Ransome books.

Roger looked nervous when Tim took out his
jackknife and placed it on a log.

"Will it hurt?" he asked.

"I don't think I want to," said Gavin.

"Don't be such cowards," said Tim scornfully.
"Look, I'll go first."

He opened up the knife and scratched the blade
tentatively on the ball of his forefinger. Then he
jabbed. Gavin closed his eyes.

But nothing happened. Tim jabbed again: two,
three, five times. But the blade was too dull to pen-
etrate his skin.

"Oh, well," said Roger. "We can just *say* a pact."

"No, there has to be blood," insisted Tim. He
rooted in his pockets and pulled out a safety pin.
"This should work." Placing the point of the pin on
the same place, he pushed slowly and withdrew the
tip. "There!" They all peered at the tiny gleam of
blood on his finger.

"Hurry!" said Tim. "Do yours before mine
dries!"

Roger took the pin and pushed it in quickly. "Ouch!" He stuck his finger in his mouth.

"Don't waste it!" said Tim. "Now you, Gavin."

Gavin held the pin over his fingertip. "Do it!" ordered Tim.

He pressed the pin into his finger. It really hurt and he withdrew it quickly. Some blood welled up and pooled along the lines in his skin.

How strange to think that his body was full of gallons of this bright red liquid. Blood *flowed*; that's what they learned in school. It meant you were alive — life blood. A gruesome thought came into his head. His parents' blood would have stopped flowing when they were killed. That was what death was.

"You can get way more if you squeeze," said Roger. They pinched their sore fingers until half a red globule hung from each one.

"Okay, rub them together," said Tim. He smeared his bloody finger over Roger's finger, then Gavin's. The others did the same.

"Now I have blood from both of you mingled with mine," said Tim, examining his finger with satisfaction.

"We should say something," said Gavin.

Roger looked solemn. "We three swear, by the mingling of our blood, that we will be blood brothers and friends forever."

"I swear," said Tim, choking with laughter.

"I swear," said Gavin fervently. "Now we really *are* like the Three Musketeers. All for one and one for all!" They were musketeers until dinner time.

X

A Surprise Visitor

The family tried to carry on as if they weren't waiting for a decision that would change their lives forever. By unspoken agreement no one talked about it, but the whole household itched with prickly suspense. Aunt Mary was overcome by spring allergies and took to her bed. Hanny served dull, badly cooked meals and sat around the kitchen morosely nursing her tea and cigarette. Norah had to study for her final exams. Sometimes Paige persuaded her to go to a movie or the canteen, but most of the time she escaped into her books. Aunt Florence took Gavin to the Riverdale Zoo on Firecracker Day. They were both relieved when the outing was over, after the strain of pretending that everything was normal.

But when June came and there was still no word

from Grandad, Aunt Florence broke the silence. "When is he going to phone?" she asked Norah angrily. "It's unbearable, keeping us in suspense like this! If he hasn't phoned by Monday I'm going to send another telegram."

"How should I know why?" said Norah sullenly. "It isn't *my* fault he hasn't phoned yet! I want to know what he's decided just as much as you do." The two of them were as antagonistic as when Norah and Gavin had first arrived, as if their four years' truce had never happened.

Gavin began to daydream so much in class that Mrs Moss had to keep him after school several times to finish his work. "Are you worried about going back to England?" she asked during one of these detentions. She looked up from her desk as he tried to concentrate on a page of long division.

He couldn't tell her his secret. He just whispered "Yes, Mrs Moss" so sadly that she let him leave.

Gavin walked home slowly, kicking at the sidewalk and scuffing his new oxfords. He didn't care. *Waiting.* It seemed that all he had done in 1945 was wait. He felt as dry and wrung-out as the twisted dishcloths that Hanny hung on the line.

Today was Monday — the day Aunt Florence said she'd send Grandad another telegram. That cheered him up a little. At least they were *doing* something.

The house was silent when Gavin got there. Hanny told him the aunts had gone out to vote in the Ontario election. "Norah's at the library. I'd like to nip out and vote myself before I start dinner. Will you be all right by yourself for half an hour?"

"Sure." After Hanny had gone, he wandered upstairs, Bosley padding behind and whining for a bite of his cookie. Gavin was rarely alone in the house. He decided to explore every inch of it, as if he had never been here before.

First he climbed on a chair and tried to open the trap door to the roof, but he couldn't quite reach it. Then he made his way slowly downwards, from Norah's tower to the musty basement.

He even ventured into the aunts' rooms, careful not to touch anything. He examined the childhood photograph of Aunt Mary and her brother Hugh, which she always kept on her chest of drawers. On her bedside table lay a Bible and a library book called *The Building of Jalna*. A watercolour picture of Gairloch hung on one wall. Surely he'd be back in that magical place this summer . . .

Aunt Florence's room smelled like the flowery perfume she always wore. It was stuffed with cushions, soft furniture, family photographs and hat boxes. Beside *her* bed was a book about the Royal Family. Almost everything in the room was pink. Being in here always made Gavin feel as if he were enveloped in a soft pink cloud of security.

As he continued his expedition through the house, its solid presence held him like a hug. If Aunt Florence adopted him he would own this house one day! He'd own part of Gairloch too. Not until he was grown up, of course.

Bosley would be dead by then. It was so unfair that dogs didn't live as long as humans. But he'd always have a springer spaniel, Gavin thought dreamily. They would all be black-and-white and they'd all be called Bosley.

After his tour he lay on the den floor, listening to "Terry and the Pirates" on the radio. Bosley's freckled muzzle rested on his stomach. Then the door knocker banged and Bosley jumped up with a warning bark.

"Shhh! It's probably, Norah, silly. Hanny must have locked the door." Gavin got up to open it.

An old man stood there. He was short and tubby, with a white fringe of hair under his crumpled hat. Heavy brows fell over his eyes and his stiff moustache was stained with tobacco. He wore a grimy suit and a bedraggled blue tie. His shoes needed polishing. In one hand he held a battered suitcase, in the other a pipe.

Gavin backed off with alarm. He must be a tramp! Tramps usually came to the kitchen door and begged for some food from Hanny. Would this man expect him to give him something? Bosley growled and Gavin put one hand on his collar.

The man stared at Gavin with a curious, searching expression. Then he said softly, "Is it Gavin?"

"Who are you?" whispered Gavin. "How do you know my name?" Suddenly the man's face looked familiar — where had he seen it?

"Don't you recognize me? I'm your grandad! I've come to take you home."

Half an hour later everyone sat in the living room, staring dumbfounded at Grandad.

Except for Norah. She pressed against her grandfather, hanging onto his arm like an anchor. Gavin would never forget the look of utter relief on her face when she'd come through the door, minutes after Gavin had awkwardly invited Grandad into the hall. She had screamed, then collapsed sobbing in his arms, as if she were sobbing away four and a half years' homesickness as well as the grief over her parents. "*Grandad!* Oh, Grandad . . ."

"There, there, my brave Norah. I'm here now. Everything is going to be all right. Just look how you've grown! Both of you!"

Norah kept hold of Grandad while they stumbled into the living room and collapsed on the chesterfield. Then Hanny and the aunts arrived. Grandad introduced himself gruffly. Aunt Mary cried out with delighted surprise. Aunt Florence stiffened, then shook Grandad's hand without a word. She stared coldly at the old man while Hanny brought them tea and stayed to listen to his story.

"A fellow I know in the navy got me onto a ship for Canada. It was a cheap passage and I've made a bit of money this year doing carpentry. It was some voyage, I can tell you! Full of war brides and babies. The whole ship reeked of nappies!" He wiped his bald forehead with his handkerchief.

"We are *so* glad to meet you after all these years," Aunt Mary said again. "Norah has told us all about you and you can tell what a comfort it is for her to see you again." She smiled warmly at Norah.

Finally Aunt Florence spoke. "You're very welcome to stay here, of course, Mr Loggin. But I'm curious. Why did you journey all this way when Norah is about to return to England anyway?"

Gavin froze; even Bosley seemed to hold his breath.

"Your request put me into such a dither, Ma'am, that I couldn't think straight. I've never been one for letters or telephones, so I decided to come over and talk to you in person about . . . this matter. But let's wait until tomorrow for that. Right now I want to catch up with these young ones."

"Of course you do!" said Aunt Mary giddily. "We'll leave the three of you alone until dinner's ready." She and Aunt Florence and Hanny left the room.

Gavin shoved piece after piece of Hanny's gingerbread into his mouth while Norah found her voice. She and Grandad talked and talked, interrupting each other with excited comments about the rest of the family.

Grandad had an English accent, of course, but he wasn't easy to understand like some of the English teachers in school. His speech was garbled and rough and Mrs Moss would have been shocked at some of the words he used. Every once in a while he stopped and stared at Norah and Gavin. "I can't believe how much you've both changed! But of course, it's been almost five years. Do you remember me, Gavin?"

"Yes, sir," lied Gavin.

Grandad laughed. "You don't have to say 'sir' to your own grandad! And listen to your accent! Norah's not as bad, but you sound like the Yanks we had in our village."

"I'm Canadian, not American," mumbled Gavin.

"Gavin!" Norah frowned at him. "You're *not* Canadian, you know that. You just sound like one."

Grandad grew solemn and talked about their parents' death and the funeral that the whole village had attended. Norah cried again. Curled up against Grandad she looked even younger than Gavin.

"It's such a damned tragedy," exclaimed Grandad. "My only daughter . . . how I miss the arguments Janie and I used to have! And Arthur, always so cheerful and calm. He never agreed with me on much, but he always accepted me." Tears formed in his sea-blue eyes.

"It's all right, Grandad," said Norah softly. "You've got us now. I'm going to quit school and take care of you."

"You'll do no such thing, young woman!" bristled Grandad. "You'll finish your education. I've heard about your good marks — it would be a bloody waste. And I'm pretty good at housekeeping, myself. Wait until you taste my meat pies, young Gavin!" He looked up at Gavin slyly. "If you search in my pockets you might find a sweetie."

When Gavin didn't respond Grandad looked embarrassed. Gavin lowered his head. A "sweetie" must be a candy. Did his grandfather think he was still five?

Was Grandad really going to take him back to England like he'd said? Was that what he was going to tell Aunt Florence tomorrow?

He glared at the grubby old man sitting on Aunt Florence's sleek chesterfield. He smelled! He used bad words! Gavin edged away from him as he and Norah talked and laughed. This *stranger* wanted to remove Gavin from the only home he had ever known.

Grandad didn't look nearly as grubby after a bath and a shave. But he still wore the shiny suit and the frayed tie at their late dinner. Gavin could tell that Aunt Florence was embarrassed to have him in the house. He thought of Uncle Reg's meticulous dark suits and snowy shirts. To Gavin's horror Grandad tucked his napkin under his chin and slurped his soup.

"A super meal," he told Hanny, as she took away his dessert plate. Hanny smiled — she seemed to like him as much as Aunt Mary did. "You wouldn't believe the food in England," said Grandad. "Rationing's getting worse instead of better. Of course the parcels you've sent us have really helped."

He glanced at the mahogany table and the silver gleaming in the candlelight. "Norah and Gavin were certainly lucky, to come to such a fine house. I'm sure they wouldn't look so fit if they'd stayed in England." He cleared his throat. "I know

Jane and Arthur would want me to thank you. We can never repay you for the kindness you've shown our young ones."

Aunt Mary dabbed at her eyes. "It was *our* privilege, Mr Loggin. They're wonderful children and it's changed our lives to have them with us for so long." She and Grandad beamed at each other. Grandad lit his pipe and puffed foul-smelling smoke into the room. Norah sniffed it in and sighed happily.

But Aunt Florence and Gavin sat stiffly in their chairs, one disapproving and the other afraid.

XI

A Decision

Grandad was put into the spare room next to Gavin's. Gavin tossed all night, his dreams interrupted by the snuffle and wheeze of loud snores.

Their grandfather was still asleep when Gavin and Norah left for school. "The poor man must be exhausted after such a long journey," said Aunt Mary.

When Grandad got up, thought Gavin, he would tell Aunt Florence he was taking Gavin back to England. By the time he got home for lunch it would all be decided.

At least they had lantern slides in school that morning. Gavin sat woodenly in the darkened classroom, while Mrs Moss's voice droned on about daily life in Lapland. Tim sneaked Gavin a package of Lifesavers. Gavin just held it in his lap, until

Martin snatched it, hissing, "What's the matter with you, Stoakes? Pass it on!"

"No talking! Remember there will be questions afterwards," warned Mrs Moss. Luckily she didn't call on Gavin; nothing from the slides had sunk in.

He thought of asking himself to Tim's house for lunch. But that would just stretch out the agony of not knowing.

When Gavin got home, however, no one was there but Hanny. She gave him a peanut butter sandwich alone in the dining room.

"Where *is* everyone?" he asked.

"Norah took her lunch as usual. Mrs O and Mary had their Red Cross meeting. And your grandfather has gone out to buy some tobacco. My, he's a card. He says I cook eggs better than his wife did!"

"Did — did he and Aunt Florence talk to each other?"

Hanny sat down beside him. "Yes, Gavin, they did. They were in the den for an hour. You're worried about your grandfather wanting you back, aren't you . . ."

"What did Aunt Florence look like when she went out? Mad?" He could picture exactly her affronted expression when she didn't get her way.

"I'm sorry, Gavin, I was doing the dishes when she left. Your grandfather seemed fairly cheerful, though, when he came in to ask me directions."

"But that's bad!" cried Gavin. "If he was cheerful, maybe he got what he wanted!"

"Now, now . . ." Hanny patted his arm. "We don't know that yet." She sighed. "It's such an impossible decision. You can understand why both he and Mrs O want you. *I'd* like you to stay, of course, but I wonder what's best . . ."

"It's best that I stay!" Gavin pushed away his sandwich and ran up to his room. If even Hanny wasn't sure he should live in Canada, maybe he wouldn't be allowed to.

"Gavin?" Hanny had followed him up. "Are you all right?"

"I feel sick." His head was whirling and his stomach felt queer. "Can I stay home from school this afternoon?"

"Of course you can. I don't know how you'd sit through it, waiting to hear the decision. Shall I bring the kitchen radio up?"

"All right."

He lay on his bed and listened dully to "The Happy Gang." Then he turned off the radio and tried to read, but soon he slept. His dreams were a jangled repetition of big hands reaching out again and again to snatch him and pull him apart. He woke up sweating. Red lines were etched in his cheek from pressing against the pattern in his bedspread.

The house was silent. Gavin crept to the door of his room and listened. Footsteps sounded in the downstairs hall and Aunt Florence's voice said, "Very well. I'll see if he's awake."

She started up the stairs, then saw him standing at the top. "There you are, sweetness! Are you feeling better? Hanny said you weren't well."

"I'm okay."

"Come into the den, please, Gavin. Your grandfather and I want to talk to you."

This was it. He followed Aunt Florence's erect back down the stairs. He couldn't tell from her voice what the decision was.

Gavin sat down in the den, his legs trembling. He was curiously relieved; at least he was finally going to *know*. Bosley lifted his head from the rug and gave his tail a sympathetic thump.

"Gavin . . ." Grandad looked as fierce as Norah did when she knew what she wanted. "As you know, Mrs Ogilvie has offered to take you permanently into her family — to adopt you." A strained politeness came into his voice. "It's a very generous offer, especially after all she's already done for you. She also says that you *want* her to adopt you. Is that right?"

Gavin lifted his head. "Yes, sir," he said clearly.

Grandad winced. "I can understand that. You've obviously been happy here and you don't remember your real home. And if you stayed in Canada you'd have a lot of advantages our family could never give you."

Hope stirred in Gavin. Was it possible that Grandad was going to agree?

But then Grandad sat up straighter. With a stubborn look at Aunt Florence he said, "Perhaps it's unfair of me to deprive you of those advantages, Gavin, but I can't give you up. Neither can Norah or your other sisters. Even though you've lost your parents, you still have us. We're your family. I know you don't remember us — but we remember *you*. We love you. You *belong* with us. So I'm afraid . . ." He wiped his forehead and carried on firmly. "I'm afraid that I can't allow Mrs Ogilvie to adopt you."

For a few seconds the room spun. "But I want to stay here," Gavin said weakly. "Please, sir — Grandad — can't you let me?"

"Gavin, old man, I know you want to stay. But you're only ten. You don't know what's best for you. You'll get used to me — *and* to England. Believe me, in a year or too you'll be glad I made this decision for you. And I *am* your legal guardian," he added, with another defiant glance at Aunt Florence. "I'm supposed to make decisions for you."

"Aunt Florence!" cried Gavin. "Don't let him take me!"

Aunt Florence's voice was low and furious. "There's nothing I can do about it, pet. We've gone over and over it all day, but he won't budge."

The two adults stared at Gavin greedily, as if they were pulling him apart — just like his dream.

Gavin jumped to his feet. "*No!*" he shouted, facing Grandad. "I won't go back with you! It's *not fair!* I'm happy *here!* I belong *here!* Why can't you let me stay where I'm happy?" Tears streamed over his cheeks, but he didn't even notice, his anger was so overpowering.

"Gavin!" Aunt Florence pulled him over to her. "Calm down! You're getting hysterical!"

"Oh, Aunt Florence . . ." Gavin buried his face in the haven of her soft front and sobbed frantically. "Aunt Florence, I don't want to leave you! I don't want to live with him! Don't let him take me away from you! *Please!*"

He kept on crying for a long time, while Aunt Florence tried to soothe him. Finally Grandad spoke, his voice broken. "Am I so awful, then, Gavin? I'm not an ogre, you know."

"I'm s-sorry," gulped Gavin. "But I don't want to leave!"

Grandad wiped his forehead again. "I can't think," he mumbled. "This room is so bloody —" he glanced at Aunt Florence — "this room is so warm."

Aunt Florence stood up and took Gavin's hand. "Your grandfather and I need to talk alone again, pet. Go and ask Hanny to bring us some lemonade. I'll call you when we're ready for you again."

Gavin stumbled out and gave Hanny the message. Hanny gave him some lemonade too, and he sipped it at the kitchen table. Hanny chattered to him about her husband's model trains; her voice seemed to come from far away.

It was a long time before Aunt Florence finally called him. Gavin made his frozen legs walk back into the den.

"Your grandfather has come to a decision," said Aunt Florence. Her face was bent and her voice so low that Gavin gave up hope.

Grandad's eyes were bleary and red. "Gavin, my boy . . . you looked at me back then just like Janie used to, when she wanted something desperately. I knew you were close to Mrs Ogilvie. But I suppose . . . I suppose I didn't realize *how* close. I don't mean to be cruel . . ."

Gavin took a quick breath while Grandad continued.

" . . . and I can't bear to make you this unhappy. Are you absolutely certain that you want to stay?"

"Yes!" whispered Gavin.

"After all, your happiness is the most important thing," said Grandad slowly, as if convincing himself. He sighed. "All right." He threw Aunt Florence a bitter look. "You can stay. But I've given Mrs Ogilvie one condition."

"What?" breathed Gavin.

"That she doesn't start legal adoption proceedings until after Norah and I have left. I want you to have that time to change your mind if you want to."

"I'll *never* change my mind!" said Gavin. Then he flinched at Grandad's hurt expression. For the first time, he felt sorry for the old man.

"You certainly seem to know what you want," said Grandad gruffly. "But remember, Gavin, even if it's the day we leave — even if it's after we're back — you can still decide to live with Norah and me, all right?"

"All right," whispered Gavin to the floor.

"Now, if you'll both excuse me, I'd like to go to my room." He walked out stiffly, holding his white head high.

Aunt Florence stared at the chair where he'd been sitting. "This is very hard for your grandfather," she murmured. "It's extremely generous of him to give you up."

A warm glow slowly filled the numb space inside Gavin. "I'm going to stay," he whispered.

Aunt Florence smiled at Gavin as if she couldn't believe her luck. "Yes, pet . . . you're going to stay!"

Gavin let out a long sigh. "*Jeepers* . . ."

"Jeepers is right!" she laughed. "That's exactly how *I* feel!"

"Can I tell Tim and Roger?"

"I don't see why not. You can tell whomever you like. But Gavin — try not to act too excited while Norah and Mr Loggin are still here. It will hurt their feelings if you're too happy about staying. Remember that you aren't going to see them for a while."

Gavin couldn't think of that. He was going to stay!

"This is going to be a difficult time," mused Aunt Florence. "Especially saying goodbye to Norah. But after that . . . oh, come over here and give me a kiss."

Her arms were shaking when she hugged him. It was as if they had been through a battle — like another kind of war. But they'd *won,* thought Gavin gleefully. He and Aunt Florence had won!

"I'm staying!" Gavin told Bosley, after Aunt Florence had also gone up to her room. He got down on the rug and tickled Bosley's stomach. "You're going to be my dog forever and ever!" Bosley licked Gavin's face, as if he wondered what all the fuss was about.

Gavin lay against the dog — *his* dog. Relief bubbled through him like warm water. He was staying. He was *safe.*

Once again he was afraid to tell Norah. But he

knew Grandad had told her already from the anguished looks she gave him all through dinner. Afterwards she invited him to go for a walk around the block.

"Grandad said you're staying," she muttered, staring straight ahead. She stopped walking and faced him. "Gavin, are you *sure* this is what you want?"

"Yes!" Why did everyone have to keep asking him that?

"I thought seeing Grandad again would make you change your mind. But you don't even remember *him*, do you?"

"No. I'm sorry."

Norah's eyes filled with tears. "I can't bear to leave you behind! You're my brother!"

"I'm sorry," said Gavin again.

"Gavin, when we left England D-dad and Mum . . . " Norah swallowed a sob. "They told me to take care of you! At first I forgot." She blushed. "I was too wrapped up in my own misery to think of you. But then when I realized how much — how much I loved you, I promised myself that I'd *always* take care of you. If I leave you here I'm breaking that promise! It's like breaking a promise to Dad and Mum! Can you imagine what *they'd* think of us separating?" Her sobs overtook her and she flung herself down on someone's lawn.

Gavin crouched beside her. "*Please*, Norah! You *have* taken care of me — good care!" He thought desperately. "But if you let me stay, then *that's* taking care of me too — because that's what I want! And

you'll still be my sister, no matter where we live."
He took her hand.

She clutched it with both of hers. "I just don't
know! I suppose you're right, in a way. I suppose
your happiness is the most important thing. It's so
mixed up. I'm so *tired*. I'm so sick of trying to decide
what's right." She let go of his hand. "I give up,
Gavin." Her voice was broken. "I can't fight you any
more. If you really want to stay, I guess Grandad and
I will just have to accept it. All I can do is hope that
you'll change your mind."

Gavin shuddered. How could he hurt her like
this? Especially when she'd already suffered so
much. But he had no choice "I'm sorry," said Gavin
for the third time, "but I won't change my mind."

"I guess there's nothing I can do about it, then,"
she said wearily. They walked back to the house in
miserable silence. Norah wasn't angry with him.
But there was a new distance between them, as if
they already lived in different countries.

XII

Grandad

"You're staying?" cried Tim.

"Forever?" said Roger.

Gavin grinned at his friends. "Yes! Aunt Florence is going to adopt me! And I get to keep Bosley!"

"Hooray!" Tim threw his baseball glove into the air, then pounded Gavin on the back.

"Now we really *are* blood brothers," laughed Roger. The three of them linked arms and continued to walk to school.

"Will you change your last name to Ogilvie?" asked Tim.

Gavin hadn't thought of that. He had been Gavin Stoakes all his life.

Before he sat down at his desk he went up to Mrs Moss and said shyly. "I'll be here again this fall, Mrs Moss. The Ogilvies are adopting me!"

"Why, Gavin! What a nice surprise! May I tell the whole class?"

"All right." He blushed when everyone clapped, but their grins warmed him. Someone passed him a folded note.

"I'm glad you're staying. I hope we'll be in the same class again next year. Eleanor." He sneaked a look at her, but she was bent over her desk.

Gavin told everyone he knew: the policeman at the crosswalk, the woman in the store where he bought gum and comics, and Miss Gleeson at the library.

"If that's what you want, I'm very happy for you," said the librarian, as she stamped out *Homer Price* for him. "But what about Norah? Is she staying too?" Miss Gleeson had been one of Norah's first friends in Canada.

Gavin flushed. "She's going back to live with my grandfather," he mumbled.

"Oh." Miss Gleeson looked surprised, but she didn't say anything else.

The more Gavin talked to people about staying, the less he had to think about Norah leaving. But he kept his promise and tried not to talk about it at home.

Aunt Florence, Aunt Mary and Hanny gave him special smiles; but more often they watched Norah desperately, as if she were disappearing before their eyes. At least Norah still had to spend most of her time cramming for exams. Then Gavin could avoid her.

Grandad, too, holed himself up. He had taken

over the late Mr Ogilvie's study. Aunt Florence had requested that he not smoke his pipe anywhere else in the house. "It's very hard on my daughter's allergies," she said stiffly. Even though she had won, Grandad's continued presence seemed to irritate her.

"But Mother, I like the smell of pipe tobacco," protested Aunt Mary. "My father used to smoke a pipe," she explained to Grandad.

"It's not good for you," repeated her mother.

Grandad seemed relieved to have a place to escape from her. When he wasn't visiting a downtown beer parlour he'd discovered, he sat in the study for hours, reading every line of the newspapers. All the way up in his room Gavin could hear the ringing tap of his pipe as he emptied it into the ashtray.

When Norah wasn't working she retreated to the study with Grandad. Talking about their parents or making plans for England, Gavin supposed. He knew he'd be welcome to join them, but he preferred to listen to the radio in the den.

"Mary, I've decided to cancel our Sunday bridge evenings for the time being," Aunt Florence told her daughter as they sat in there one evening.

"But Mother — why?" Aunt Mary was an avid bridge player.

Aunt Florence glanced at Gavin. He pretended to be absorbed in his book. "I don't think Mr Loggin would feel comfortable with our friends," she murmured.

"But he's a delightful man!" said Aunt Mary.

"And don't you think they'd be interested in hearing about England?"

"That may be, but I've made up my mind."

Aunt Mary looked as if she'd like to protest, but as usual she didn't dare. From then on none of the Ogilvies' usual friends visited the house — as if Grandad were something to be ashamed of. Gavin knew Aunt Florence was being snobby. But he told himself that Grandad probably didn't want to meet her friends anyway.

"What are you up to today, Gavin?" said Grandad one Saturday morning. "I thought we could take in the pictures, and have a bang-up tea somewhere afterwards."

"The pictures?" said Gavin.

Grandad smiled. "The movies, to you. How about it?" He almost looked afraid as he waited for Gavin's answer.

Gavin thought fast. "Uhh — I was going to do something with Tim and Roger today."

"They could come too! Ring them up. I'll treat you all."

There was no choice. Tim and Roger were both delighted that they didn't have to pay for a movie. They pressed beside Grandad on the streetcar, listening avidly while he told them how his house had been bombed by the Germans in the summer of 1940.

"That's why I ended up living with my daughter's family. I'll never forget the look on your mother's face when I turned up at the house!" he said to Gavin. "They took me in with no hesitation."

Gavin sat quietly while the other two plied Grandad with questions. Norah had often talked about the time Grandad had arrived so unexpectedly on their doorstep; that was the day before their parents told them they were going to Canada.

Gavin had been there too, of course — but he couldn't remember it at all. He wondered if his mother had felt as surprised and shocked then as he had when Grandad appeared at the Ogilvies' door.

And had the old man really been wanted? His parents' letters had sometimes complained about Grandad: spending all day in the pub, never wiping his feet, arguing with his son-in-law about the American soldiers. Gavin glared at his grandfather. Why did he have to keep turning up uninvited, disrupting other people's lives? If he hadn't come, maybe Norah would have decided to stay after all.

They went to see *A Tree Grows in Brooklyn* at Shea's. Gavin liked the first part the best, when Francie and her brother Neeley — who looked just like Tim — ran wild around the slums of New York. But after the father died, the movie got uncomfortably serious. Francie's sharp grief was just like Norah's. When she finally cried, Gavin felt guilty all over again that he never had. He looked around the audience. All the adults were sniffling, including Grandad.

"What a fine picture!" said Grandad when it was over. He wiped his eyes. "Did you boys like it?"

"It was okay," said Roger. "Except for the soppy parts."

"I liked it when Neeley said 'cut the mush,'" grinned Tim.

"The family reminded me a bit of *our* family," said Grandad. "The way they made do in a hard time."

Was their family that poor? wondered Gavin. If so, he was even gladder he wasn't going back.

They walked along the crowded sidewalk. Tim and Roger were squeezed ahead and Gavin was stuck beside Grandad.

"I didn't realize the film was about a death," he said. "I hope it didn't bother you too much. I'd better warn Norah not to see it."

"There's Murray's," pointed out Gavin. He ran ahead to catch up with the others.

"Is anyone hungry?" Grandad asked when he reached them.

"I am!" cried Tim.

They went inside and each had a milkshake and as many doughnuts as he wished. Tim managed four.

Gavin was surprised at how easily shy Roger talked to Grandad. He began telling him about his father. "He might be home next week! Mum has all his favourite food ready for him."

"And you haven't seen him since you were seven?" said Grandad. "Do you remember him?"

"Of course I do!" said Roger. "The week before he left he taught me how to play chess. Every time he writes he says I'll probably beat him in our first game." Roger stopped eating and sat in a happy daze. Gavin had never seen him look so carefree.

He sipped his milkshake jealously. Lucky Roger. He had a father and he sounded nice. Tim's father was nice, too. He always had time to throw a ball with Tim and his brothers.

Would he have remembered *his* father when he finally saw him in person? But it was too late to wonder about that now. His father was dead. All he had was this grandfather who had tried to yank him away from a family and a place he loved.

"Your grandfather's swell!" whispered Tim on the way home. "He said he'd send me a piece of shrapnel when he gets back! You must feel real sad that he's leaving soon."

Gavin shrugged. "Hey, wasn't it great when Francie and Neeley got the Christmas tree?"

Grandad kept on trying to make friends with Gavin. He invited him into the study, but Gavin stayed there for as short a time as possible, then made up an excuse to leave. Still, he took Gavin to the museum and to Casa Loma.

"No wonder you like this city," he said. "It's so clean and modern. You should see London — it's a mess of bombed-out buildings. I wish I had time to see some of the rest of Canada. You and Norah are lucky children. You've been west and to Montreal and a cottage in the north every summer."

The worst part of spending time with Grandad was that he went on and on about Ringden and the family there. He seemed to expect Gavin to know about things like cricket and pig clubs. "Muriel and Barry's house is only a few minutes away from

Little Whitebull," he told Gavin. He chuckled. "Your nephew Richard is a real bruiser. He looks like his Dad but he has the Loggin stubbornness. Like Janie and Norah — like me! When Richard doesn't want to eat something he clamps his lips closed."

Gavin grunted a reply. Why would he be interested in a baby?

"Do you remember your friend Joey?" continued Grandad.

Gavin shook his head impatiently.

"You and he were inseparable. He's a bit of limb, Joey is. Just before I left he got into a lot of trouble for breaking a window in Mrs Chandler's house."

"I don't remember him," Gavin repeated.

Often Grandad gave him a sad, pleading look. Then he'd say *sneaky* things. "Ringden's a great place for young ones. You can run wild there — hardly any cars and lots of woods to play in. And there's always Gilden to go to for the pictures. When our house is rebuilt I was thinking we could get ourselves a dog. Joey's mother has a pointer cross who's expecting pups."

Grandad was trying to bribe him! And he'd *never* have a dog that wasn't a springer spaniel.

He can't make me change my mind, Gavin thought. Grandad wasn't the only one who could be stubborn.

Gavin developed a hacking cough that wouldn't go away. He felt well enough, but he sounded terrible. Aunt Florence made him stay in bed for two days. As always when he was sick, she brought him special food and new toys and read to him for hours.

"How are you feeling?" Grandad stood at his door on the morning of the second day.

Gavin made himself cough weakly. "All right, I guess."

"This is quite a room you have," said Grandad. He came in and glanced at all of Gavin's stuff. "English kids haven't been able to get toys for quite a while."

Was that *his* fault? He wished Grandad would leave; this was the first time he'd ventured into the one place Gavin could escape from him.

"You don't seem very sick to me," said Grandad quietly. "These women coddle you too much."

Gavin glared at him. "I *am* sick! The doctor said so."

Grandad just raised his bushy eyebrows. He dropped a new comic on the foot of Gavin's bed and left without a word.

XIII

Mick's Plan

The social worker phoned and said Norah could sail on a ship that left on July 13. Grandad would have to pay his own way, but there was space for him also.

"But that's only four weeks away!" cried Aunt Mary. "Oh, Norah, I can't bear it . . ." She stifled a sob.

"Now, Mary, we knew it would be short notice," said Aunt Florence. "I certainly don't want you to leave so soon, Norah, but who knows when another sailing will be available? And Dulcie and Lucy are going on the same ship — that will be pleasant for you."

"I'm sorry it's so soon too — but it's what we planned," said Norah. Her eyes shone with excitement but she avoided looking at Gavin.

"I'm going to have a large farewell party for

you," said Aunt Florence grandly. "You can ask whomever you like — your whole class, if you want!"

"Really?" Aunt Florence didn't approve of many of the teen-agers in Norah's class. "*Thank* you!" Norah looked daringly at her guardian. "Can we roll up the rug for dancing?"

"I suppose so," smiled Aunt Florence. "But leave sitting space for the adults."

She and Aunt Mary began to pack a trunk for Norah. Every day Aunt Florence brought something home for her. "I want you to be the best-dressed girl in Ringden." Norah didn't even object that she hadn't picked out the new clothes herself. Gavin was amazed that she and Aunt Florence, now that they were parting, were suddenly so easy with each other.

Aunt Florence hardly paid any attention to Gavin — as if she were putting him off until later. Gavin knew he should be spending as much time as he could with his sister; he wouldn't see her for a long time. But he still couldn't talk to her. And all Norah seemed able to do was to give him the same yearning looks that Grandad did. Gavin kept on avoiding both of them.

His relief at staying in Canada had turned sour. Guilt gnawed at him constantly, as if he had a small wild animal living inside him. He tried to reason the guilt away. If he left he'd make five people miserable — Aunt Florence, Aunt Mary, Hanny, Tim and Roger. Not to mention Bosley. By staying he was only hurting Norah and Grandad. And surely after they left this guilt would disappear. Aunt Florence would focus on him again and he'd be safe.

The reasoning didn't work. He skulked around home and school like a criminal.

"What's eating *you*?" complained Tim, when Gavin snapped at him for accidentally ramming into his bike.

"Quit worrying, Gav," smiled Roger. "He didn't even scratch it."

Roger was blissful these days. His father was back and every afternoon Roger ran home to play chess with him. And Tim had just got a dollar in birthday money. He had endless, gloating discussions about what he'd buy with it.

Gavin scowled at his friends. Why did they have to be so cheerful?

"I get to go on a shi-ip, and you do-on't!" taunted Lucy one morning in the schoolyard.

"I don't *want* to go," retorted Gavin. "I'd rather stay in Canada."

"But you're English, not Canadian!" said Lucy. "The Milnes don't think it's right that Mrs Ogilvie is keeping you here."

"She's not keeping me! I *chose* to stay!"

"Well, I think you should come back with us. We all came over together — we should leave together, too. I can hardly wait to see my family." She looked at Gavin curiously. "Of course, it's different for you when your parents aren't there any more. But don't you want to see Ringden again?"

"Just leave me alone!" Gavin turned his back on her, only to face Eleanor.

"I'm having a birthday party this Sunday, Gavin," she said. "Would you like to come?"

"I don't go to parties with girls," he answered stiffly.

"Then don't come!" She flounced away.

Why had he said that? It was as if someone else had said it.

Then he found out that Eleanor had asked Tim and Roger too. They pretended to be scornful but Gavin could tell they were pleased. Only six boys, including Gavin, had been invited. It was the first mixed party in grade five.

"*I* wouldn't go to a sissy girls' party," Gavin told his friends at recess. Maybe he could change their minds.

"I'm only going because Tim's going," Roger protested.

"And I'm only going because Eleanor's mother is such a great cook!" said Tim. "Remember that cake she brought last year?"

"You're going because you're *sissies*," pronounced Gavin. "A musketeer wouldn't go."

Roger turned pale. "If you feel like that, maybe we shouldn't be blood brothers any more. Right, Tim?"

"Right!" muttered Tim. There were hurt tears in his eyes. The two of them left Gavin standing alone.

He kicked at the dirt. *Now* what had he done? In only a few minutes he had alienated his best friends.

I don't care, he told himself.

"Hey, Stoakes." Mick was slouched by the bike

stand, watching him. "Come over here."

Mick was back to his cruel self these days; Doris had laughed at him in front of her friends. Once again, everyone stayed out of his way.

But Gavin made his feet walk over. He met Mick's eyes and tried to sound cool. "Yeah?"

Mick's ugly mouth sneered. "Wanna make a few fast bucks?"

"How?"

"I have a plan, but I need someone to help me with it. If you do I'll give you a share of the profits."

"What is it?" whispered Gavin.

"Meet me here after school and I'll tell you."

For the rest of the day Gavin wondered if he would. Mrs Moss scolded him for forgetting his blackboard monitor duties. When he said sullenly, "It wasn't just *my* fault. Marit forgot too," she frowned at him. "That's not like you, Gavin. You know Marit was sick for half the week." Gavin almost wished she'd keep him after school so he wouldn't have to meet Mick, but she just looked disappointed and told him to fill the inkwells.

When he came to Eleanor's desk she deliberately shoved his arm. Blue ink splattered over the desk, Gavin and Eleanor, and the floor. The class snickered.

Then Mrs Moss was really cross. "Gavin! What's wrong with you this week?"

"It was Eleanor's fault," Gavin tried to tell her, but she made him get a wet rag from the janitor and clean up every spot.

By tattling on both Marit and Eleanor, Gavin had broken the most sacred class rule. For the rest of the day no one spoke to him. He remembered when the class had acted like this towards snooty Colin. Now he knew how Colin must have felt. Hurt. *Angry.*

If no one in 5A liked him any more, then he might as well do what Mick wanted.

After school he waited by his bike, watching Tim and Roger get on theirs and ride away without a word. All the other bicycles were gone by the time Mick appeared.

His leering face actually looked pleased. "So you came. I had to write stupid lines, or I would have been here sooner. Follow me. I'll explain on the way."

Gavin didn't dare ask where they were going. He walked his bike and tried to keep pace with Mick's long legs. He hoped no one noticed him. And he hoped that this wouldn't take too long. He was supposed to report home first before he went anywhere after school, and it was already late.

"Okay, here's the deal." Gavin had to strain to hear Mick's low voice. "You know Sullivan's Hardware on Yonge Street?"

"Uh-huh."

"There's an old dame who works in there. I want you to go and chat her up while I look over the goods."

"What do you mean?" asked Gavin.

Mick looked impatient. "Women *like* kids like you, Stoakes. They think you're cute. So go in there and talk to her. Ask her for something and get her into a long conversation. In the meantime I'll stash one of those expensive fishing reels in my pocket. Don't stop talking until after I've left the store. Then just go home. I'll sell the reel — I know a guy who'll buy it — and I'll give you, say, a third of the price, okay?"

Gavin stopped walking. "But that's stealing!"

Mick glared at him. "*Yes*, Mister Goody-Goody, it's stealing. But I'm the one who's doing it, so you don't have to worry your pretty head about it. All you have to do is sweet-talk the lady for a few minutes and you'll get some cash." He sniggered. "After all, I sort of owe you, don't I?"

Was he right? Was it only Mick who would be stealing? Gavin *pretended* he was right. A sick kind of excitement filled him, replacing the guilt.

Why not do something wrong for a change? Everyone — Aunt Florence, Aunt Mary, Mrs Moss — thought Gavin was good. But he wasn't. He was letting his sister go away without him.

He reminded himself of what Mick had done to Roger. But a reckless voice inside him said, "I don't care."

"So, do you have enough guts to do it?" asked Mick. "Or are you as yellow as you look . . .?"

"I'll do it," said Gavin quickly.

Mick slapped him on the back and looked friendly again. "Good for you, Stoakes!"

"But what if you get caught?"

"I've *never* been caught," boasted Mick, making Gavin wonder how many other times he had stolen something. "But if I am, just pretend you weren't with me. I'm the one who's taking the risk. *You* have nothing to lose."

They turned up Yonge Street. "So, kid . . ." said Mick, in an interested voice.

Gavin looked at him with surprise. "Yeah?"

"So how do you like being an orphan?"

Gavin shrugged.

"I'm an orphan, too, you know. My folks were killed in a car accident in Nova Scotia."

"When?"

"Five years ago. I lived with my grandfather but he died too. So I had to move to this rotten city and live with my aunt. All she does is holler at me and she never gives me any money."

"Oh." Why was Mick telling him all this? Mick looked as if he wondered too. He spat on the sidewalk. Gavin worked up some saliva in his mouth and spat too. Mick gave him a sudden, warm grin.

They reached Sullivan's Hardware. Gavin had often noticed it when he'd gone to the library, but he'd never been inside. Mick ordered him to park his bike by the door. Gavin needed more time to think, but Mick shoved him inside.

Just as Mick had said, an older, white-haired woman was sitting on a stool behind the counter. She looked up from her knitting and smiled at Gavin. "Hello, dear."

"Hello," Gavin squeaked, trembling so much he could hardly answer. But his fear made her warm to him.

"Don't be shy. May I help you?"

"I want —" Why hadn't Mick given him enough time to think of something? Gavin looked around desperately at the tool displays and lawn mowers. Behind the counter were dozens of open bins full of nails and screws.

"I need some . . . nails," he said.

"What kind of nails, dear? As you can see, there are lots of sizes."

"Umm . . . about this long." Gavin held his hands a little way apart. The woman laboriously got down from her stool and picked some nails out of a bin. Gavin could hear Mick entering quietly behind him. "This size?"

"Those are a bit too long." Gavin made her go back three times to pick another size. But the old woman was wheezing so much he couldn't ask her again.

"These are okay," he said. He paused. Out of the corner of his eye he could see Mick prowling the fishing section.

"I need them for my costume," he said wildly.

"And what costume is that?"

"There's a costume parade on the last day of school."

"That sounds like fun. Do you go to Poplar Park?"

"No, Prince Edward. I'm going to the parade as — as Sir Launcelot, so I need to make a sword." Suddenly inspired, Gavin added, "My dog, Bosley, is going as my horse."

The woman laughed. "Bosley! That's a funny name."

Now Gavin had no trouble talking to her, for he no longer needed to lie. He chatted easily about how Bosley had been already named when he got him, and how he had been a borrowed dog but now belonged to Gavin permanently. When the woman found out he'd come over as a war guest she asked him the usual questions about how he liked Canada. "I suppose you'll be going home soon," she said.

"Actually, I'm staying in Canada. That's why I get to keep Bosley. My parents were killed in the war so the family I've been living with is adopting me."

Her kind eyes filled with pity. "You poor dear! What a lot you've been through!"

Gavin suddenly realized that Mick had left the store. "Um, I have to go now," he said, turning to leave.

"But what about your nails?"

"Oh, yes." Gavin dug in his pockets, than flushed. "I'm sorry — I forgot my money. I'll come back for the nails later."

"It's such a small amount." The woman smiled. "Take them now, dear, then you can get started on your sword. You can come back tomorrow and pay me — you look like an honest little boy."

"No, that's okay." Gavin tried not to run out. Once he was outside he took a deep breath to steady his lurching stomach. He hopped on his bike and rode home as fast as he could.

"Gavin! Where have you been?" asked Aunt Mary as soon as he came into the hall.

"I — I had to stay after school again," mumbled Gavin.

"But you should have phoned and told us, the way you usually do!"

"I'm sorry. Please don't tell Aunt Florence."

Aunt Mary looked grave. "All right. But it's not like you to be naughty. And I'm worried about how many times you've been kept after school this term. Is something wrong?"

Gavin shook his head and escaped to his room. "Naughty" sounded so tame. Stealing and lying weren't naughty; they were *wrong*.

All the same, he was filled with a strange, defiant exhilaration. He and Mick hadn't been caught, and he'd done the most daring deed in his life. He'd been as brave as a knight, he thought proudly, the way he'd talked to that woman without faltering. Wait until he told Tim and Roger! Then he sighed. Tim and Roger weren't speaking to him.

He wondered if Mick really would give him some of the money. If he did, Gavin would buy a whole lot of comics and gum and invite Tim and Roger over to share them. Maybe then they could be blood brothers again.

XIV

Hot Water

Gavin sat in class the next afternoon colouring a map of the British Isles. "Make England red, Wales purple, Scotland yellow, the Irish Free State green and Northern Ireland orange," Mrs Moss instructed.

Why those particular colours? wondered Gavin. Ordinarily he would have asked the teacher, but now he just filled in England with his red pencil crayon. Colouring was soothing, like being back in grade one.

He was especially careful when he got to the area where Kent was. A year this summer he'd be visiting Norah there. He'd be eleven and a half then and going into grade seven, maybe to a fancy boys' school. Norah would be sixteen! Would she look the same?

Someone knocked on the door and Mrs Moss took a piece of paper from a messenger. She read it and looked up. "Gavin . . . Mr Evans would like to see you in his office."

Gavin froze. The whole class stared at him, the way it always did when someone was in trouble.

"Run along, Gavin," said Mrs Moss gently. "He probably wants to talk about your staying next year. Carry on with your work, everyone."

Gavin forced his legs to stand up and take him out the door. Maybe Mrs Moss was right, he thought frantically.

His steps resounded on the wooden floor. The office seemed miles away, unlike the time he had sped along the same corridor to announce the end of the war.

When he reached the outer office his slender thread of hope snapped. Mick was sprawled on the bench where you waited to see the principal.

Gavin sat down beside him, his pulse pounding in his throat. "Hi, Mick," he whispered.

"Shut up, Stoakes," Mick growled. "Just remember — we were each on our own."

Gavin didn't have time to think or reply. The secretary came out of the inner office and said, "Mr Evans will see you both now."

She closed the door behind them. They had to stand side by side in front of the principal's desk. He sat behind it, leaning back in his chair, his usually absent-minded face intent with anger.

"I've called the two of you in to discuss an incident that occurred in Sullivan's Hardware after school yesterday. Mrs Sullivan noticed a fishing reel missing after two boys had been in the store. She said the younger boy talked to her while an older boy came in. The younger boy said he went to Prince Edward School."

How could I be so *stupid*? thought Gavin.

Mr Evans cleared his throat and leaned forward. "She also said that the younger boy was a war guest. Therefore I have no doubt at all that the boys were you two. Gavin, you are the only war guest of that age left in this school and Mick, you're rather accomplished at this sort of escapade, are you not? What I *don't* know is whether this was a set-up. It certainly looks like it. But I find it very hard to believe, Gavin, that a boy like you would do such a thing. Did you? Or did you just happen to be in the store the same time as Mick . . .?"

Gavin could say that. He knew Mr Evans would believe him — he *wanted* Gavin to be innocent. Although the principal was remote, he had always been kind.

Gavin remembered the friendly way Mick had talked to him on the way to the store, and how Mick was an orphan like he was. He remembered a phrase he had heard once: "honour among thieves." He knew Mick wouldn't tell on him.

But why should Mick get all the blame?

"Well, Gavin, I'm waiting."

Gavin hung his head. "Yes, sir. I — I helped Mick steal the fishing reel."

"I'm deeply shocked, Gavin." He turned to Mick. "Do you admit to this crime?"

"I have to, don't I?" muttered Mick. "Now that he's squealed on me."

Gavin gasped. That wasn't what he'd meant to do!

"This is the last straw for you, Mick," said the principal. "You are out of this school. I've given you enough chances. I don't want your kind here to influence younger boys. Go and wait outside. Your aunt will be here shortly. *And* a policeman. We'll talk again when they both arrive."

Mick slouched out. Gavin tried to catch his eye. I'm sorry! he wanted to plead. Then he looked at Mr Evans and began to tremble.

"You're in very hot water, young man. Sit down over there." Gavin sat in the chair Mr Evans waved to. Was he going to have to see the policeman too? Would he be put in jail?

Mr Evans seemed to read his mind. "You're lucky, Gavin, that you're not going to be involved with the police as well," he said sternly. "But you have such an unblemished record that they said I could deal with you myself."

Gavin waited to be dealt with. But instead of being stern, Mr Evans's voice became kind — so kind that Gavin's tears spilled over.

"I know you've had a difficult time this term," said the principal. "Your parents' death and your guardian's decision to adopt you must have disrupted you considerably. But do you understand what a terrible thing it is that you've done?"

On and on went his tired, disappointed voice. "Yes, sir," whispered Gavin at intervals. He wanted to sink into the floor with shame. Sir Launcelot or a musketeer or the Shadow would never have stolen — *or* betrayed someone. On the radio the Shadow always said that crime didn't pay — he was right. Gavin promised never to steal again. He apologized tearfully over and over until Mr Evans seemed satisfied.

"All right. I believe you, and I know that you would never have done it if Mick hadn't put you up to it. However . . ." Mr Evans's voice was stern again. The principal was pulling open a drawer in his desk, the drawer that every boy in the school dreaded . . .

"You know that I can't let you get away with this without punishment, Gavin. Stand up, please, and hold out your hand."

Gavin didn't think he *could* stand up, his legs were so wobbly. His hand shook just as much. Mr Evans came around the desk holding the strap. Gavin had never seen it but it was familiar from other boys' descriptions: thick, black and rubbery, about the length of a ruler.

He was hit six times on each palm. His hand sunk under the force of each blow, but Gavin knew you were supposed to bring it up again on your own, or else the principal would hold your wrist. Finally it was over. Gavin couldn't stop blubbering as he frantically rubbed his stinging palms against the sides of his pants.

"All right," said Mr Evans gruffly. "Go to the boys' washroom until you've calmed down. Then go back to your classroom. I'm going to have to phone Mrs Ogilvie and tell her about this. But I don't want to hear that you've talked to anyone else about it, do you understand? The matter is closed."

Outside the office Mick was sitting beside a sour-looking woman and a grave policeman. Gavin scuttered past them, hanging his head to hide his tears.

He rushed into the boys' washroom, sat in a cubicle and sobbed. Then he held his flaming, puffy hands under cold water until they felt a bit better. He splashed water on his face too and slowly walked back to the classroom.

After you got the strap you were supposed to grin while you swaggered back to your seat. Gavin couldn't manage it. Everyone murmured with surprise when they noticed his hands. "Back to work, class," said Mrs Moss, but she looked as shocked as the rest of them. Gavin bent over his map but his throbbing fingers couldn't grasp the pencil crayon.

At recess he was surrounded. "What did you *do*?" they all asked.

Gavin reddened. "I'm not allowed to say."

"How many times?"

"Six on each hand."

"Wow . . . the most I've ever had is three," said Tim. "Meet Roger and me after school, okay?" he added in a whisper.

"Okay," said Gavin gratefully.

When they lined up to go in Eleanor came over and demanded to look at his hands. "Strapping's so mean!" she shuddered. "And it's not fair that only the boys in this school get the strap when the girls don't. Are you *sure* you don't want to come to my party, Gavin?"

"I'll come," said Gavin, trying to return her smile.

Mrs Moss kept him after school for a few minutes. "I've heard all about it, Gavin," she said quietly. "I'm sorry you had to be punished. I think you know that Mick has been permanently suspended."

"What will happen to him?" asked Gavin.

"He'll go to a special school." Mrs Moss sighed. "Maybe they can help him."

It's my fault he had to go, Gavin thought. But it wasn't really. Mick would likely have been caught even if Gavin hadn't squealed; if not for this incident, for something else.

He would probably never see Mick again. He thought once more of the strange bond between them on the way to the store.

On the way home Gavin told Tim and Roger a condensed version of the robbery. He knew he could trust them not to tell anyone else.

"I can't believe you did it!" said Tim, half-horrified and half-admiring.

"Why did you?" said Roger. He seemed more certain than Tim of the enormity of Gavin's crime.

"I don't know," said Gavin. "I guess I just wanted to see what it was like. But I never will again!" he added sheepishly.

"Want to come over to my house?" Tim asked.

Gavin shook his head. It was a comfort to have his friends back, but now he had to face the music at home. What if Aunt Florence was angry too?

XV

Leave Me Alone

Norah was modelling a new coat for Aunt Florence and Aunt Mary in the den. The three of them greeted Gavin so normally he knew Mr Evans hadn't phoned yet. He decided he might as well tell them first.

Slowly he stuttered out the whole story. Aunt Florence's stout figure shook with fury as she listened. Then she pressed Gavin's wounded palms between her large, plump hands. "How *dare* someone hit you!"

"I didn't think old Evans would ever strap *you*!" said Norah. "Did it hurt a lot?"

Gavin nodded and Bosley put one paw on his knee.

"First thing in the morning I'm going to go to the school and give that man a piece of my mind!"

snorted Aunt Florence. "He has no right to hit you! Especially when it was Mick's fault, not yours!"

"Why didn't you *tell* me about Mick?" fumed Norah. "I could have done something about him! Is that who you had to get the money for in December?" Gavin nodded again.

"What money?" demanded Aunt Florence. "What else has this Mick done?"

In a halting voice Gavin told them about the money, then about Roger being left naked in the ravine.

"But you should have told us!" cried Aunt Florence. "You poor little boy, putting up with him all this time!"

"Imagine letting a bully like that stay in the school! Someone who forces younger boys to help him steal!" shuddered Aunt Mary.

"It's completely unjustified!" said her mother. "Gavin should never have been punished. I'm going to demand that Mr Evans *apologize* to you, pet — to you *and* to me."

"Hold it!" said Grandad. Gavin didn't realize he'd come into the room. "I think we're getting things a little out of proportion here."

"What do you mean?" said Aunt Florence coldly. "Gavin has been *struck*!"

"I heard," said Grandad quietly. "And I'm sorry he has. But listen to me for a minute, Gavin. This is the usual punishment at your school when someone does something wrong, am I right?"

"Yes," whispered Gavin.

"So it seems to me the question is whether or

not you deserved to be punished. Do you think you did?"

Gavin gulped at how stern Grandad's eyes looked under their bushy brows. "Yes, sir."

"He *didn't* deserve it!" cried Aunt Florence. "That boy *made* you go along with him, didn't he?"

Gavin started to agree. Then he looked back at Grandad. "No, Aunt Florence. I didn't have to do it."

"But you'd never do such a thing of your own free will!"

"I did, though," said Gavin, wincing at the shocked expression that came into her eyes.

Everyone was quiet while they digested this. "But *why*, Gavin?" Aunt Mary finally asked.

"I don't know. I just . . . did! I promise I never will again," he said to Aunt Florence.

She bridled. "Well, you may *think* you chose to — to steal — but I don't believe it! That boy brainwashed you! And no child of mine is going to be strapped! I'm still going to ask Mr Evans to apologize to you."

"But —" Gavin could well imagine her marching into the school and giving Mr Evans a "piece of her mind." He'd never be able to face his classmates again.

"I can't let you do that, Ma'am," said Grandad.

Aunt Florence looked as if she hadn't heard properly. "What did you say?"

Grandad's voice was low but angry. "I won't let you embarrass my grandson by saying anything to his principal. In the first place he *isn't* your child

— not yet. And you heard what Gavin said. He was wrong. He knew very well what he was doing — he could have refused. I don't believe in hitting children myself, but we have to accept the school's methods. Gavin deserved his punishment. And after school tomorrow he and I are going to that hardware store so he can apologize to the owner."

"He is *not*!" cried Aunt Florence. "Why should he have to suffer any more than he has? He's coming to Mr Evans's office with me first thing in the morning!"

"No!" Gavin wondered who had shouted so loud, then realized it was himself. He glared at Aunt Florence and shook with anger. "I don't *want* you to go to his office, Aunt Florence! Everyone will laugh at me if you go! And Grandad's right — I *did* steal! I'm not always good! I'm *tired* of being good! Stop treating me like a baby! Just — just *leave me alone!*"

He was still shouting, standing in front of her and clenching his fists.

Aunt Florence wilted against the cushions of her chair, as deflated as if he had poked her with a pin.

"Thatta boy, Gavin!" whispered Norah. They all waited for him to continue. But his fury had fallen as quickly as it had risen. "Please, Aunt Florence," he continued wearily. "Please don't say anything to Mr Evans."

"Very well, Gavin," said Aunt Florence stiffly. "If that's what you want, we won't discuss the matter any further." She marched out of the room.

Never, in the whole time since Gavin had known her, had she spoken to him so coldly.

Grandad met Gavin after school the next day. It was raining and the gloomy weather added to Gavin's dread as they approached the hardware store.

"What shall I say to her?" he asked outside the door.

"Just say you're sorry."

"But she might be really mad!"

"I wouldn't be suprised if she was," said Grandad. "Would you like me to come in with you?"

"Yes, please," said Gavin.

He kept as close to Grandad as possible as they went over to the counter. The woman looked up, then frowned.

"So it's you."

"I'm very sorry I helped Mick steal the fishing reel," said Gavin as fast as he could. But his tongue was like a piece of wood and his words came out fuzzily. "It was wrong. I promise I'll never do it again."

"How can you expect me to believe you? And to think I thought you were such an honest-looking boy! I won't be fooled like that again, I'll tell you!" She scowled at both of them. "And who's this?"

"My grandfather," said Gavin, taking Grandad's hand. The skin on it was rough but warm.

"Huh! I bet he's pretty ashamed of you."

"If my grandson says he'll never steal again he won't," said Grandad quietly.

"Don't be so sure." She glared even harder at Gavin. "You'd better be careful you don't end up in reform school like that other boy! Get out of my store! I never want to see you in here again!"

Gavin pulled Grandad out of the store. "She wasn't very nice!" he said when they got outside.

"Well, you weren't very nice to *her*, were you? She's angry because she trusted you and now you've betrayed that trust."

Gavin sniffled and Grandad handed him his handkerchief. "Never mind, old man. You've apologized — that's the most important. You were brave. I'm proud of you." Gavin kept hold of his hand all the way home.

"I'm sorry I shouted at you, Aunt Florence," said Gavin that evening. She hadn't spoken to him all day.

Aunt Florence's voice was remote and sad. "I accept your apology, Gavin. Perhaps I was slightly precipitate."

Gavin didn't know what "precipitate" meant. She didn't call him "pet" the way she usually did. "Pet" *was* an awfully babyish nickname, though . . .

"Give me a kiss and run along, then." She held out her cheek but she didn't add a hug the way she usually did.

After that Aunt Florence did what he'd asked her to — she left him alone. She was as polite and distant to him as if he were a visitor.

Gavin wondered if he really wanted this. It was like standing in a bright open field instead of in a

protective forest. He could tell she was still hurt by
his words. But surely, after Norah and Grandad left,
her old easy affection would return.

All weekend Gavin sat in the study with his
grandfather and sister. They were leaving him alone
as well; they no longer made him feel pressured to
change his mind. Like Aunt Florence, they seemed
afraid to upset him.

As usual Grandad and Norah talked about
home. Little Whitebull the way it used to be . . .
Ringden with its shops, cricket green and sur-
rounding hop-fields . . . various people in the village
. . . and, of course, their family. As Gavin listened,
faint outlines of these places and people formed in
his mind. He didn't know whether he was remembering or imagining.

"I feel sorriest for Tibby," said Grandad,
"because most of her things were still in the house.
Do you remember the watercolours she used to do,
Norah? They were all lost."

"She painted a picture of a cow," said Gavin
suddenly. "With brown spots."

"Gavin!" cried Norah with delight. "*I* remember that picture! She painted it for *you*! For your fifth
birthday!"

Gavin scrunched up his face to hold onto the
memory, but it sank back into his mind as quickly
as it had bobbed up.

The next day, though, a few more things came
back to him — like a blurry film coming into focus.
He remembered the tinkle of the bell in the village
shop and the sour smell of the scullery in their

house. When he told this to Norah and Grandad they hugged him.

"Oh, Gavin . . ." said Norah, but Grandad gave her a warning glance.

The three of them chatted together quietly, enjoying their fragile new harmony. No one dared mention they only had three weeks left together.

XVI

The Birthday Party

That Sunday Gavin, Tim and Roger walked slowly along the sidewalk to Eleanor's house.

"*How* many boys are going?" Roger asked again.

Gavin counted on his fingers. "Us three, Jamie, George and Billy."

"And *all* the girls," groaned Tim.

"I don't think I'll come after all," said Roger when they reached Eleanor's house.

Gavin tugged him up the steps by his sleeve. "Come on, Rog. All for one and one for all!" He banged the knocker before Roger could flee.

Mrs Austen stood in the doorway, an apron over her dress. "My, don't you all look spiffy! Let's see . . . I know Tim from church. Are you Roger?" Roger nodded shyly. She put her hand on Gavin's shoulder. "Then you must be the poor little English boy who lost his parents — Gavin, isn't it? Come and join the others in the living room."

Now Gavin wanted to leave too, but they had to follow Eleanor's mother along the hall.

Fourteen girls were crowded together on one side of the living room, whispering to each other. Jamie, George and Billy sat silently on the other side.

Gavin sneaked a look at Eleanor after they had joined the other boys. Like all the girls she wore a fluffy dress and had a large bow tied on one side of her head. Her dress had tiny pink flowers dotted over it. He had never seen her hair loose before. It waved around her face.

The only sounds were stifled giggles from some of the girls. Eleanor looked as if she wished she hadn't decided to have a mixed party. Gavin tried to catch her eye and reassure her.

Mrs Austen bustled back into the room. "What's all this shyness about?" she cried, with a silly, tinkling laugh. "Let's have a game and break the ice!" She clapped her hands. "Everyone into a big circle!"

They all had to stand in a circle as if they were three years old. Gavin manoeuvred himself so he was next to Eleanor.

"Hokie Pokie!" cried Mrs Austen. "You put your right hand in, you put your right hand out ..." She flung her hand in and out in time to the tune. No one sang, and only two girls copied her.

"You put your left hand in . . ." She faltered, then stopped singing. "I guess you don't know that one. Sit down where you are and we'll play Button, Button."

Mrs Austen reached into her pocket and showed them a small white button. "Now, who wants to be It?"

When no one volunteered, she looked at her daughter. "How about the birthday girl!"

Eleanor blushed. She took the button from her mother and knelt in front of each person in turn. "Button, button, who's got the button?" she muttered, placing her palms together and passing them through each person's praying hands.

Gavin smiled at her when she reached him and she gave him a tiny smile back. Then she opened her hands slightly and let go of the button. He pressed his palms against it tightly.

"Can anyone guess who has it?" asked Mrs Austen.

"Gavin," said Tim accusingly. He must have seen their exchanged smiles.

Gavin opened his hands to reveal the button.

"Good for you, Tim! Now you're It."

Gavin grinned as poor Tim had to touch each of the girls' hands. He knew he would give the button to Roger; but he didn't want to guess and have to be It next. Everyone else refused to guess too.

Mrs Austen sighed. "Well, if you're tired of Button, Button, I have another game. Don't go away!" She hurried out of the room and returned with a tray filled with small objects. "Kim's Game! I'll give you five minutes to memorize the contents."

This was better; they could separate into boys

and girls again while they examined the tray. Gavin had always been good at Kim's Game. He concentrated hard: an apple, a pair of scissors, a china cat, a handkerchief . . .

Mrs Austen took the tray away and they each tried to remember its contents. Roger got them all and won a small bag of candy.

"Now that was really fun!" said Mrs Austen, flushed with success. "How about London Bridge?"

"Please, Mum," begged Eleanor. "Can't we stop playing games and open the presents?"

Mrs Austen looked disappointed. "No more games? All right, then, sweetheart."

They sat on the floor around Eleanor while each person handed a present to her in turn. The girls all began talking as if they were by themselves, oohing and ahhing at the hair ribbons, necklaces, small dolls and ornaments that Eleanor unwrapped. The boys sat forgotten at the edge.

"Why do girls like such boring stuff?" whispered George. "My mother bought her a pincushion!"

"Mine got her a comb and brush set," said Tim scornfully.

Gavin smiled to himself. He had chosen Eleanor's present himself: a copy of his favourite book, *Lassie Come Home*.

"Thanks, Gavin!" Eleanor looked over at him when she had unwrapped it. "I've seen the movie but I've never read the book."

"The book's just as good," he assured her.

Mrs Austen stood at the door. "Everyone into the dining room!"

"At last!" whispered Tim.

Eleanor blew out the eleven candles dotted over the large chocolate cake. Mrs Austen helped her cut it and passed cake and ice cream to everyone.

"Have you all had enough?" she asked after second and third helpings. They looked up from their scraped plates and grinned at her.

"Now you can go back into the living room and amuse yourselves until it's time to go home," said Mrs Austen. She looked relieved as they filed out.

Once again the girls and boys sat on separate sides of the room. But their full stomachs made them relax. Jamie let out a noisy belch and everyone laughed. Suddenly they acted ordinary, as if they were in the classroom.

"Do your blushing trick, Tim," said Sylvia.

Everyone watched Tim while a slow pink wave ascended from his neck to his forehead.

"How do you *do* that?" asked Wendy.

Tim shrugged. "I don't know. I've always been able to do it."

"Hey, can anyone do this?" Billy bent his fingers backwards. "I'm double-jointed," he boasted.

Then George showed them how he could make his arms rise on their own by standing in the doorway, pressing his wrists against each side of it, then letting go. Everyone had to try.

"Can we see your monkey, Eleanor?" asked Corinne. They followed Eleanor to her room where Kilroy crouched in a cage, glaring at them with beady black eyes.

"He's mad because he's locked up," said Eleanor.

Gavin looked curiously around her room. There were the usual girls' things — dolls and frilly curtains — but he noted with approval that she had a microscope and many of the same books that he had.

"Let's play Murder In the Dark!" suggested Charlotte.

"It's not dark enough," said Eleanor.

"How about Sardines?" said Lizzie. "I'll be It. Is it all right if I go anywhere in the house?"

"Anywhere but the kitchen," said Eleanor. "Then we won't bother Mum."

Lizzie ran out to hide. The rest of them sat on the bed and the floor in Eleanor's room, counting to one hundred in unison. Then they fanned all over the house to search for her.

Gavin tried the basement, the den and the living room before he heard faint giggling coming from Eleanor's parents' bedroom. He ventured in and discovered Lizzie, Charlotte, Jamie and Frances under the bed. He squished in with them and stifled his laughter while they watched Tim's feet come into the room and go out again.

By the time ten of them were crammed under the bed they were giggling so much that the rest had no trouble finding them — except for Tim. When he was the only one left they screamed his name until he came back into the bedroom. "But I *looked* in here!" he grumbled.

"Charlotte's It," said Lizzie. "She was the first one to find me."

"What's all this?" Mrs Austen came into the bedroom. "Now, Eleanor, I really don't think you need to be in here. If you all go back into the living room I'll bring you some ginger ale."

Everyone sprawled in friendly comfort in the living room, gulping down the welcome drink.

"Do you know who I saw the other day?" asked Marit. "Miss Wright! She was in Woolworth's and guess what she was buying — an eraser!"

They all shrieked with laughter. Old Miss Wright had been their grade three teacher. Every day she had confiscated someone's eraser and a rumour had started that she ate them after school.

"Do you think we'll get Miss Mackay or Miss Hood next year?" asked Shirley.

"Miss Hood's *really* mean," shuddered Frances.

"Maybe we won't get either of them," said Eleanor. "Mrs Moss told me there'll be a bunch of new teachers next year, especially for the older grades — men who've come back from the war."

"A man teacher! That'ud be swell!" said Tim.

"Did you know that soon we'll have *television* in Canada?" asked Meredith.

"I know about television," said Roger timidly. It was the first time he'd spoken. "Everyone will have a screen in their living room with sound and pictures."

"My mother says it won't last," said Jean. "You have to look at it all the time. You can't do other things, like when you're listening to the radio."

"And you have to make the room really dark," said Wendy.

"And the screen's really tiny," said Gloria. "Why would anyone want to watch a tiny little screen when you can go to the movies? Did anyone see *The Three Caballeros*?"

Gavin leaned against a chair, listening to the chatter. They were all friends with him again. Most of them had been in his class since grade one. Now that he was staying in Canada, they'd be in his class next year as well.

"I have an idea," said Sylvia. "Let's dance!"

"Dance?" cried some of the girls with excitement.

"Dance?" said Tim in horror.

"Okay," said Eleanor. "My sister has lots of records, and we just got one of those automatic record players." She went over to it and in a few seconds Doris Day was crooning "Sentimental Journey."

Sylvia drew the curtains and turned off the lights. Some of the girls retreated to a corner, but others looked determined. "Come on, Jamie. Come on, Billy." They dragged the boys into the middle of the room and pulled them around in the dim light.

Gavin backed away from Meredith and quickly turned to Eleanor. "Would you like to dance?"

In a few minutes even Roger was dancing. The other girls danced with each other, giggling as someone stepped on a clumsy foot.

Gavin steered Eleanor carefully. He had practised dancing every summer with the older cousins at Gairloch. "You're good!" whispered Eleanor as someone put on "There, I've Said It Again."

"Isn't there something faster?" complained Joyce, but Gavin was glad he could still hold onto Eleanor. Her hand was soft and she smelled like Ivory soap.

Mrs Austen hurried in. "Dancing! Don't you think you're too young for that? It's time to go, anyway. Mrs Anthony is here to pick up Jean and here comes Mr Everett up the walk."

Gavin and Roger and Tim walked home, past lawns sparkling with greenness in the hot June air.

"That wasn't *too* bad," admitted Roger.

"The grub was super!" said Tim. He'd stuffed his pockets with peanuts and they nibbled them as they walked.

Gavin just smiled, thinking of how Eleanor's hair had brushed against his cheek.

XVII

The Farewell Party

Mrs Moss gave up on regular lessons for the last few days of school. Instead 5A listened to her read *Tom Sawyer*. They also helped clean the classroom, by taking down the maps, perfect spelling papers and drawings pinned up on the walls and sweeping out and scrubbing the ledges, floors and desks.

On the last afternoon Mrs Moss stood in front of them holding a sheaf of white cardboard. "I'm happy to tell you that everyone has been promoted to grade six," she smiled. She passed out the report cards in order. Eleanor, as usual, was first, then Roger.

The class examined the report cards as Mrs Moss poured out glasses of lemonade. Gavin had good marks in English and socials but he only got 61 in arithmetic. He was afraid to look at conduct, but to his relief he got a B. Underneath Mrs Moss had scribbled, "Gavin has bravely overcome the difficulties he's had to endure this term. We are delighted he will be back with us for the next school year." She didn't say anything about him getting the strap.

Gavin looked up at his teacher, as she merrily chatted with the girls who were helping her pass out cookies. If he were marking *her*, she'd get all A's.

After the treats were finished and the empty glasses collected, each pupil waited to be released.

"You'll always remember this school term," said Mrs Moss. "The term the war ended. Now it's up to your generation to grow up and make a world where there *aren't* any wars."

There was a solemn silence while the class digested this. Mrs Moss looked apologetic. "What long faces! You don't have to do it *yet*. Enjoy being young first! I've liked teaching you very much," she continued. "I hope you all have a wonderful summer and come back ready to work hard in the fall."

Tim writhed with impatience. "Three cheers for Mrs Moss!" he shouted. He jumped to his feet and everyone else followed. "Hip Hip *Hooray!* Hip Hip *Hooray!* Hip Hip *Hooray!*"

"Thank you!" Then at last came the phrase they'd been longing for. "All right . . . you may go."

Everyone rushed out the door, lugging book bags and calling back goodbyes to Mrs Moss.

Mr Evans smiled at Gavin, Tim and Roger as they passed him in the hall. "All ready for your holiday, boys?"

"Yes, sir," they mumbled, slowing their run to a walk. Gavin avoided the principal's eyes. He would never be able to forget what nice Mr Evans had done to him.

A chant echoed all over the playground:

No more pencils
No more books!
No more teacher's
Dirty looks!

"What are you doing this summer, Gavin?" Eleanor stood by the bike stands as Gavin tried to fit his bulging schoolbag into his basket.

"We're going to the cottage like we always do," said Gavin. "But this year we have to wait until after . . ." He swallowed. "Until after my sister and my grandfather go back to England."

"When's that?"

"July the thirteenth."

Eleanor glanced at Tim and Roger approaching and said quickly, "I'll be in Toronto all of July. Maybe you could come over before you go to the cottage."

"Maybe," said Gavin. "See you, then."

"See you." She rushed away to join her friends.

"What did *she* want?" said Tim.

"Oh . . . she just wondered what I got in English," said Gavin.

"She always beats me in that," muttered Roger. "If it wasn't for English, *I'd* have the highest marks."

Their bags were so heavy they had to walk their bikes, balancing the loads on their handlebars.

"This is the fourth best day of the year," pronounced Tim. "First is Christmas, then your birthday, then Hallowe'en — then today! Let's ride our bikes to Hogg's Hollow tomorrow."

"We're leaving tomorrow," Roger reminded him. He and his parents were going to stay with relatives in Collingwood for July. Roger's father had been told to take a complete rest. "He wakes up at night shouting," Roger had told them. "He dreams he's still fighting. And sometimes he just sits in a chair for hours, not saying anything." He looked as anxious as he had before his father returned.

"I guess we won't see you until September, then," Gavin told Roger as they neared the corner.

"I guess not. Have a good summer. 'Bye!"

"I'll come over tomorrow after breakfast," Tim told Gavin.

After they separated they each turned around and shouted, "All for one and one for all!"

On Dominion Day Gavin and Tim went to see *Son of Lassie* at Loew's. Gavin had been longing to see it but he couldn't pay attention. All he could think of was Norah leaving.

Ten more days, ten more days . . . The refrain pounded relentlessly in his head. A week from Friday Norah and Grandad would go to Union Station to catch the train to Montreal. They'd stay overnight with the Montreal relatives, then continue to Quebec City, where they would board a ship called the *Strathern* for Liverpool.

"Are you all right, Gavin?" asked Aunt Mary a

few days later. She sat down on the stairs beside him. He had moped there since breakfast, staring at Norah's trunk packed and ready in the hall. Today it was going to be picked up and shipped ahead of her.

Gavin shrugged, and Aunt Mary put her arm around his shoulder. "Even though we've been prepared for this for so long, I still can't believe the time has almost come."

They were quiet for a few minutes. "You can still change your mind if you want to," said Aunt Mary softly.

Gavin looked at the trunk. It stood near the closet he used to play in when he was younger, pretending that the late Mr Ogilvie's canes were horses. The silver bowl on the side table and the red Persian carpet glowed in a beam of sunlight. Very soon the trunk would be taken away from this peaceful hall that smelled of roses. It would start its long journey to an unknown country. "No!" he shuddered.

Aunt Mary pulled him closer. "As long as you're sure. I certainly don't want to lose you — not you as well as Norah." She sighed. "Soon you and I and Mother and Hanny will be at Gairloch. That will cheer us up."

"And Bosley," whispered Gavin, as the dog nudged his knee. "You'll be glad to get to Gairloch, too, won't you boy?" Bosley had been lying sadly by the trunk all week.

"Where is Norah?" asked Gavin. "I haven't seen her all morning."

"She went downtown with Mother to buy a new dress for the party."

At least getting ready for the party gave them all something to do. Hanny and Aunt Mary spent hours in the kitchen. Gavin helped Norah move back the furniture and roll up the rugs.

"I hope Paige remembers all her records," she said. How could she think about records at a time like this?

Aunt Florence continued to be distant with Gavin, but she put on such a good act of being affectionate that no one but Gavin knew how much she'd changed. Norah and Grandad, on the other hand, could scarcely let Gavin out of their sight. Grandad took him to Centre Island for the day and Norah even dragged him over to Paige's with her. Now they talked about what they'd do when Gavin visited England next summer.

"We'll go to Camber, of course," said Grandad. "Wait until you see the beach — miles and miles of sand! When you were a little tyke you used to bury me in it."

A dim memory of holding a tin pail and shovel tugged at Gavin's mind — then let go.

"Andrew is coming to visit me for sure!" Norah told them. "I sent him Muriel's address. He says he has a surprise — for all of us! You'll probably see him at Christmas, Gavin."

Grandad went upstairs for more tobacco. "Norah, what will happen with you and Andrew?" blurted out Gavin.

"What do you mean?"

"Will you — will you *marry* him?" He shivered. If Norah had to live so far away, he wanted her to stay exactly the same.

Norah grinned in the carefree way she used to before their parents' death. "Marry him! I'm only fifteen!"

"But I thought . . . "

She blushed. "I know I told you I loved Andrew. But I was different . . . then. Now I don't expect anything from him. I still like him a lot. But he's probably changed — just like I have. I'm just going to wait and see how I feel when I see him."

Grandad came back and began telling them how he planned to add a new room to the house. "For you, old man," he smiled. "It will always be there for your visits."

"When you come next summer I'll show you where I saw a crashed German plane," said Norah.

How could they chatter on so cheerfully, when they were going to leave so soon? Then Gavin heard the pain in their voices. They were only pretending to be cheerful; pretending for him.

The family sat in the living room, waiting for the guests to arrive. The house was spotless and the dining-room table was heaped with food and drink. It was a hot night and Gavin's short wool trousers itched. Norah looked much older than fifteen in her new yellow-and-white polka dot dress and bright lipstick. Even Grandad was dressed up, in a clean shirt and a blue tie. He fanned his sweating face with the evening paper. With an exasperated look at Aunt Florence, he fingered his empty pipe.

"I can't believe you'll only be with us for five more days, Norah!" said Aunt Mary, fumbling for her handkerchief.

Aunt Florence frowned at her. "Now, Mary, none of that. Here's someone arriving," she added with relief.

Paige and her sisters and parents filled the hall. "Do you want me to show you how to do an Chinese burn?" Daphne whispered to Gavin. "I take your arm and . . ."

"No!" he said, backing away from her. If only she were Eleanor. Aunt Mary had asked him if he wanted to invite his friends, but he'd shaken his head. After all, the party wasn't for him.

More and more people filled the house. It was just like after the memorial service — but now everyone was laughing instead of acting solemn. Gavin scowled. Why were they all so cheerful? Norah and Grandad were *leaving* — that wasn't a reason to celebrate!

The adults — friends of the Ogilvies and a few of Norah's teachers — sat on the furniture around the edge of the living room. Teen-agers danced on the cleared space in the middle. When there was a slow dance some of the adults got up and joined it.

Gavin tried the jitterbug with Norah and the foxtrot with Aunt Mary. Daphne and Lucy kept asking him to dance. He refused, but he couldn't shake off Daphne. She followed him everywhere and never stopped talking. Finally he sat nursing a Coke while Daphne stood in front of him, describing in gloating detail how she'd almost been expelled from her school after she filled her teacher's desk drawer with worms.

"I don't know how Paige is going to *exist* without Norah," Mrs Worsley was telling Aunt Mary behind them. "She's wept buckets of tears all week."

"We're hoping Norah can visit Toronto in two years," said Aunt Mary. "We'll go over there first next year, and then she can come here. If we carry on taking turns, at least we'll see her once a year. And that will keep her in touch with Gavin." She lowered her voice. "Sometimes I feel it's wrong, separating them. I know it's what Gavin wants, but I still wonder . . . I don't know how he's going to bear saying goodbye to his sister."

Gavin ducked his head as the women looked at him. He watched Norah teach Grandad how to jitterbug. The two of them were laughing so hard they could hardly stand up.

How could they laugh?

Gavin glanced back at Daphne; now she was talking to her mother. Very carefully he slipped out of the living room. He tiptoed across the hall, then ran up the carpeted stairs to his bedroom.

Bosley stuck his head out from under the bed. "Poor Boz," said Gavin. "You don't like the party either, do you? I don't blame you. It's a *stupid, boring* party . . ." He sat on the floor in the dark, leaning against the bed. Bosley emerged all the way and rested his heavy head on Gavin's leg. The party noises floated up from below: talking and laughter and the jaunty melody of "Mairzy Doats."

Tears slipped down Gavin's cheeks. Bosley struggled to his feet and licked them away.

Gavin clutched him. He was all alone ... except for Bosley. Norah and Grandad were leaving him. But that was his fault. He had chosen to stay in Canada to be safe.

But he didn't *feel* safe any more. The big old house, which had always been such a secure fortress, seemed empty and cold, as if Norah had already left. And Aunt Florence, who had been an even safer haven, had changed. That was his fault, too. He had driven her away with his anger.

Now he heard "Three cheers for Norah, Dulcie and Lucy!" Then the voices began singing "We'll Meet Again."

"Oh, Boz ..." Gavin squeezed the dog again, but so tightly that Bosley whined in protest and went back under the bed. Gavin crawled in after him. Maybe he'd feel better where it was dark and confined.

He hadn't been under his bed for years. It reminded him of hiding under Eleanor's parents' bed. That time he'd been happy, squashed in with his friends.

Now he just felt silly. His bed wasn't as high as Mr and Mrs Austen's; he could barely raise his head. Bosley watched curiously while Gavin slithered around on the bare floor, trying to get comfortable. Finally he managed to turn over on his back. He stared at the mattress bulging between the springs. His tears dribbled into his ears.

Then he stopped crying. On the far side of the

bed, against the wall, a lumpy shape was squished between the spring and the mattress. Gavin slid himself over, reached out his arm, and forced his hand between the wires. He closed it around a small wool form, something he knew very well. As gently as he could he tugged it out — Creature!

He scraped his head in his haste to get out. Then he sat on the edge of the bed, brushing off the dustballs from his worn, stuffed toy elephant.

"Creature . . ." whispered Gavin. The elephant must have been stuck between the mattress and the wall, and worked itself under the mattress when the bed was changed. He stroked Creature's grimy trunk. He looked just the same: both his ears were missing and his tail had worn to a frayed string.

Gavin curled up on the bed, rubbing Creature against his cheek the way he used to when he was little. Creature smelled the same too — a mixture of musty wool flannel and sawdust.

A sharp image came to him, like a movie in his mind. He was sitting in a little room holding his elephant up to his face and sniffing him, the way he was now. Sitting in a high, hard chair, swinging legs that didn't reach the ground, while two grown-ups told him solemnly that he was going with Norah on a ship to Canada.

Mum and Dad. He could *see* them. Mum's tired face struggling with tears and Dad's trying to be cheerful.

". . . and remember old man," Dad's voice was saying, "whatever happens, I want you and Norah to stick together like glue! Promise?"

"I promise," whispered five-year-old Gavin.

Gavin bounced into a sitting position and tried to remember more. But that was all. The rest was a confused blur of going on a train and a ship and another train, the way it had always been.

But he remembered them! He focused on the scene again — his parents breaking the news to him as they all sat in the front room. There was a faint odour of ammonia in the air, mixing with Creature's smell. Mum wore a faded blue blouse. *Muv* . . . that's what he called her then. Her hands were red and chapped from always washing dishes. Her hair fell into her eyes. Dad had a long nose like Norah's and a warm, reassuring voice. He called him "old man" like Grandad did. Muv called him "pet" like Aunt Florence.

Gavin pressed Creature to his cheek as he held on to the memory-picture. Then his parents' images dissolved. He remembered them — but they were gone. They were dead. He would never see them again.

"*Muv* . . ." Gavin turned over and sobbed into his pillow, still clutching Creature. "Dad . . ."

He cried for a long time, until his insides were light and empty. Then he dried his face on his pillowcase and stumbled to the window. Some of the guests were leaving.

"Goodbye, Norah! Have a safe journey!"

Gavin leaned out the window and the night air cooled his hot cheeks.

"I want you and Norah to stick together . . ."

Finally he knew what to do.

XVIII

We'll Meet Again

Gavin had stumbled out of his clothes and fallen into bed and a deep, thick sleep. He woke up all at once, full of energy. It was only six o'clock.

He stuck his head into the hall. Everyone's door was closed and the usual snoring came from Grandad's room. They went to bed last night and forgot about me! he thought indignantly. But maybe he'd already been asleep when they'd come upstairs.

Gavin put on his dressing-gown, put Creature in his pocket, told Bosley to stay, and padded up to Norah's tower. Her new dress was flung over a chair and she was buried under her blankets. It was a shame to wake her, but he couldn't wait.

"Norah!" He touched her shoulder.

She groaned and shook his hand away, burrowing farther in.

"Norah, wake up!"

Norah opened her eyes halfway and gazed blearily at him. "What do you want? What time is it?"

"Six o'clock."

"Six! Go *away* . . ."

"*Norah* . . ." Gavin giggled as she put her hands over her ears. "Listen, I have to tell you something! It's really important!"

Finally she struggled awake, leaning against the headboard and yawning. "What could be so important at six in the morning?"

Gavin grinned and climbed onto her bed. "Oh, nothing. Just that I'm coming back to England with you . . ."

"*What*?" She leaned forward and clutched his arm. "Really?"

"Really and truly," he laughed. "I've decided to go back with you and Grandad."

Norah looked stunned. "But you were so sure you wanted to stay here! What made you change your mind?"

Gavin shrugged. "I just did. I can't — I just can't let you go without me. We have to stick together! Like glue! Dad told me that before we left. I promised I would, but I forgot for a while."

"But are you sure you can give up Aunt Florence and Aunt Mary? And your friends, and this house . . ." Norah looked afraid to believe him.

"I'm sure," he said. "I'm very, very sure. I want to stay with *you*. It's where I belong. And we have to take care of each other, like Muv and Dad asked us to."

"Muv . . . that's what you used to call her," said Norah softly. "Oh, Gavin . . ." She hugged him. "Look at me, I'm crying! I was wishing so much you'd change your mind but I'd given up hope! I'm so *happy!*" she said in wonder. "I never thought I'd feel really happy again." She wiped her eyes. "Wait until Grandad hears!"

"Let's tell him!"

The two of them crept hand in hand down the stairs to Grandad's room. "Listen to him snore!" chuckled Gavin.

Grandad woke up quickly. He leaned against his pillows while Gavin told him. Then his old face broke into a wide grin.

"You're coming with us?" he cried. "My dear boy . . . what wonderful news!" There were tears in his eyes. "You've made a very brave decision, old man."

Old man . . . Gavin heard Dad's voice again and smiled at his grandfather.

"I think it's the right decision," said Grandad slowly. His face became serious. "But since I've been here I've seen how much you love the Ogilvies — especially Mrs Ogilvie. It's going to be hard for you to leave them."

Not as hard as leaving *you*, thought Gavin, looking at Grandad and then at Norah.

"England's in a sorry state right now," continued Grandad. "The food is scarce and terrible. You can't buy new clothes or toys. We'll be squashed at Muriel's, then we'll be living in a half-finished house that would fit into the living room of this house. And we don't have much money. You'll have to try for a scholarship to grammar school."

"I don't care!" said Gavin.

"Can you give up all this?" Grandad waved his hand around the room — at the spool bed, ornate wallpaper and mahogany wardrobe. "This fancy house? And the summer one?"

"And you'll have to leave Bosley behind," said Norah gently. "Did you remember that?"

Gavin gulped. Why were they trying to discourage him?

"I know that! Bosley will have to go back and live with Uncle Reg. But he likes Uncle Reg. I know it will be hard — but it won't matter as long as I'm with you. Don't you *want* me to come?" he added tearfully.

"Of course we do!" they cried.

"We just wanted to make sure you'd thought about it carefully," said Grandad. "But I can see that you have. Thank you," he said gruffly. "Thank you for choosing us."

Gavin and Norah climbed onto the bed and sat cross-legged on the foot of it. The three of them beamed at each other.

"Will Gavin be able to get on the same ship?" asked Norah.

"We'll enquire about that first thing on Monday morning," said Grandad. "If he can't we'll cancel our ship and all go together on a later one."

"How am I going to tell Aunt Florence?" shuddered Gavin. "I think she's already mad at me."

"It won't be easy," said Grandad. "But we'll be with you all the way."

Gavin pulled out his elephant.

"Creature!" cried Norah. "Where did you find him?"

"Trapped under the mattress," grinned Gavin.

"I'd forgotten all about your elephant," murmured Grandad. "Your Grannie made him for you when you were born, just before she died. She would be glad you still have him. He's as old as you are! He certainly looks the worst for wear. What happened to his ears?"

"He looks fine!" said Gavin indignantly. Then he laughed with them. "I'm going to keep him forever and ever and give him to *my* children!"

Gavin knew he had to tell Aunt Florence as soon as possible. He decided to wait until after church. All through the service he daydreamed, trying to find the best words. He only paid attention when Reverend Milne asked the congregation to say a prayer for Dulcie, Lucy and Norah. "We have been privileged to have the care of these fine children for the past five years," he said, gazing sadly at Dulcie and Lucy in the front pew. "We wish them a happy future and a safe crossing to England."

"Yeck! How embarrassing!" muttered Norah.

"That prayer is for you as well, Gavin," whispered Grandad.

Then Gavin's favourite hymn was announced: "To Be a Pilgrim." "He who would valiant be /

'Gainst all disaster," he sang out. A pilgrim was sort of like a knight or a musketeer, he decided.

Gavin couldn't eat his lunch. "Are you sick?" asked Aunt Mary.

"I'm not sick." He looked at Aunt Florence. She had touched hardly any of her meal either. "Aunt Florence . . . I need to talk to you in private."

"Very well." Aunt Florence's voice was icy as she and Gavin went into the den and shut the door.

Gavin looked around at the comfortable, cluttered space. So many important things had happened in this room. Their arrival, the news of their parents' death, his decision to stay . . . He thought of all the evenings he'd spent in here listening to the radio or to Aunt Florence read. Then he remembered the valiant pilgrim and took a deep, steadying breath.

"Well?" Aunt Florence sat down heavily in her favourite deep armchair. Her voice was shaking. Then she looked at Gavin and he realized that she knew what he was going to tell her.

"Aunt Florence . . . I'm so sorry . . . but —"

"It's all right, Gavin." He'd never heard her sound so defeated. "You want to go with them, don't you?"

Gavin nodded. How could he hurt someone so much? "How did you know?" he whispered.

"I've seen how you've been clinging to Norah and your grandfather in the past few weeks. I've seen how you've changed. I think I've known ever since the day you got into trouble at school. You've been growing apart from me. I should have encouraged you to talk about it but I just — I just couldn't! Come over here . . ."

Gavin came closer and she took his hand. "I love you dearly, Gavin. I hope you know that. You've been like a son to me. But you *aren't* my son. Perhaps I've tried to hold on to you too much."

"You haven't," sniffed Gavin. "You've made me happy."

"I'm glad of that. But you don't need me any more. The war is over. And even though you've lost your parents, it's still right that you go back. It was selfish of me to try to keep you here."

She looked like a tired old woman. "Aunt Florence," whispered Gavin. He pushed into the chair beside her and the two of them sat together in silence.

The next day, after a morning of frantic telephone calls, a space was found for Gavin on Norah and Grandad's ship. Now there were only three days left. Aunt Florence seemed relieved to spend all that time doing Gavin's packing.

Gavin told Bosley he was leaving him. He wasn't sure if Bosley understood his words, but he certainly understood the open suitcases and piles of clothes in Gavin's room. He followed Gavin every-where, gazing accusingly at him.

"You'll be all right, Boz," Gavin told him. "Uncle Reg loves you just as much as I do." He had read once that dogs didn't have long memories. Bosley would probably forget all about him.

But he'd never forget Bosley.

There was so little time for goodbyes. Some of the family friends who had been at the party dropped by with small gifts for Gavin when they heard. But others didn't even know he was going — Mrs Moss, all the people in his class, and Roger. Gavin thought sadly of how casually he'd said goodbye to Roger when he thought he'd see him again in September. At least there were two people he could say goodbye to in person — Tim and Eleanor.

Tim's face turned red without him willing it to as he stared furiously at Gavin. "But you said you were *staying*!"

"I changed my mind."

"But *why*? You're Canadian, not English! You don't even talk like someone who's English! You said you didn't even remember England!" They were lying on the floor in Tim's room; Tim kicked one of his bedposts.

Gavin sighed. "I know I don't remember it. I don't *want* to leave you and Roger. I don't want to go back, but I have to stay with my family — my real family. Don't you see?"

"I thought the *Ogilvies* were going to be your real family now!"

"I thought so too, but I was wrong."

They lay in silence, Tim's face buried in the rug. Gavin knew he was hiding his tears. "I'll write to you, Tim," he said desperately. "And the summer after next, Norah and I will probably come back for a visit."

"You'll spend it in Muskoka like you always do," Tim muttered into the rug.

"Well, you can come! You and Roger! You can both come up north for the whole summer, okay?"

"I guess so . . . I like Gairloch." Tim had come for a week last year. "But that's two years away — that's forever!" He looked up at Gavin, tears gleaming on his round face. "All for one and one for all, eh?"

"All for one and one for all *forever*," said Gavin.

Eleanor was more difficult; he had to lose her just as she was becoming a friend. It would be easier to just leave without telling her. Gavin kept putting off phoning her but he finally made himself do it the day before they left.

"May I please speak to Eleanor?"

"Just a minute — *Eleanor!*" a voice shouted in his ear. Her older sister.

Then Eleanor answered. "Hello?"

"Uh — this is Gavin."

"Hi, Gavin! Are you having a good summer?"

He had meant to tell her on the phone but as soon as he heard her voice he wanted to see her one more time. "Can I come over? Right now?"

"Sure. Why does your voice sound so funny?"

"I'll tell you later."

Gavin ran all the way to her house. His shirt was sticking to his heaving chest by the time he got there.

"Let's go into the back yard," said Eleanor after she answered the door. "Mum made some lemonade."

Gavin drained two glasses of lemonade while

Eleanor sat quietly in a chair and watched him.

"So what did you want to tell me?" she asked finally.

He stared at her. Her braids were pinned around her face in a circle. It made her look like a flower.

"I came to say goodbye," he mumbled.

"Oh, you're going up north. But I'll see you in September."

"You *won't!*" said Gavin, close to tears. "I'm going back to England. I decided not to stay in Canada. My sister and grandfather and I are leaving tomorrow."

"Oh." Eleanor's expression didn't change.

"I may come back and visit Canada in a while, though," said Gavin.

"We'll be older then," she said matter-of-factly.

"Uh-huh." Maybe when they were older he'd know how to talk to her more easily. "I'll write you a letter," he said.

"Okay." Eleanor still looked as calm as if Gavin were only going away for the summer.

"So . . . goodbye, then."

She just sat there. Didn't she care at all? "Goodbye," she mumbled, staring at the grass.

Gavin walked away quickly. His legs quivered as he stomped to the front of the house and along the sidewalk.

"Wait!" He was almost at the corner when Eleanor reached him. He turned around and she stood in front of him, trying to catch her breath. One of her braids had come loose. "Good luck, Gavin," she said gravely. "I'll never forget you." She leaned forward and kissed him lightly on the lips. Then she walked away.

Gavin watched her go. Her lips were soft, like tiny cushions, and they tasted of lemonade.

That evening everyone spoke in tender, careful voices, as if afraid the other person would break. Hanny made Norah and Gavin's favourite foods for dinner. Then they sat in the den quietly, listening to a concert on the radio. Every once in a while Aunt Florence or Aunt Mary or Grandad would ask each other if some item or another had been packed.

When the concert was over Gavin fiddled with the radio dial, wondering what the programmes were like in England. Then the door knocker sounded and everyone was relieved when the Worsleys marched in noisily.

"I have a present for you, Gavin," whispered Daphne. Gingerly, Gavin took the small box she handed him. It probably contained something disgusting.

But to his surprise Daphne had given him the jackknife she always carried with her. "It's to protect you in England," she grinned. "You never know what wild animals you'll meet there. You can use it to skin them."

"Thanks, Daphne!" said Gavin. "I'll take good care of it."

When the Worsleys got up to go everyone was crying, especially Paige. "Oh, Norah, I can't bear it! You're the best friend I ever had!"

Norah wiped her own eyes. She took Paige's arm. "I'll walk home with you — then we'll have a little more time."

The rest of them went back into the den. Aunt Florence opened up *Sunshine Sketches of a Little Town* and began to read. She had begun it earlier in the month to try to cheer everyone up. But although the words she was reading were amusing, her voice was not. Gavin stared at her strong face and at Aunt Mary's gentle one.

"Excuse me," he murmured, and slipped from the room. He went into the dim living room and curled up on the window-seat.

Bosley hopped up beside him and collapsed in a silken pile at his feet. Gavin stroked him all over, from his smooth head to the ends of each of his fluffy feet, memorizing every freckle and patch. Bosley rolled over on his back with pleasure and Gavin tickled his stomach in the place he liked best. Then he pulled Creature out of his pocket. He was much too old to carry him around the way he used to, but tonight he needed him.

Glancing out the window, he saw all the street-lights come on together. He had never seen that happen before. It was like that song, "When the Lights Go On Again."

The war was over and the world's lights could shine again. That was good, of course; but the light was cruel as well as hopeful. It exposed all the bad things that had happened in the war — all the suffering. His parents crushed under their house, soldiers dying in the mud . . . and those mysterious, terrible bodies in *Life* magazine.

Gavin shivered. Tomorrow he had to venture into that glaring new world. He had to leave behind the people and places he was so used to — that he loved. Bosley whined, and Gavin kissed the white streak between his eyes. Then he huddled against the warm dog.

He couldn't do it. He would go back into the den and tell them he was staying. In two days he and Bosley could be out in the canoe at Gairloch. He was only ten. How could he be expected to give up so much? He *would* stay.

"Gavin? Are you all right?" Grandad came into the dark room and sat down beside him.

"I'm scared," whispered Gavin.

"That's understandable," said Grandad. "You're leaving everything that's familiar to you. But *what* are you afraid of?"

"Of England — and the war — and people getting killed like Muv and Dad — of everything!"

"The war's all over now, Gavin," said Grandad gently. "You know that."

But England had always meant the horror of war. It was so hard to believe that the horror wouldn't still be there.

"What else are you afraid of?"

"Starting a new school."

"That's scary," agreed Grandad, "but you've always done well and made friends in school here. I don't see why it should be any different in England. It'll *seem* different for a while, but you'll soon get used to it. Anything else?"

Gavin stroked Bosley's head. "Everything ahead is so — so *blank*. I don't know what's going to happen! It's so hard! Having to leave everybody, not knowing what it'll be like."

"Life *is* hard, old man. I'm sorry the war has made you have to find that out so soon. And nobody *ever* knows what's going to happen." He chewed on the end of his pipe. "That's what makes life interesting! I can't tell you there won't be bad times, but I promise you there will be lots of good times too. Think of this as an adventure!"

An adventure . . . like the pilgrim fighting his giants, or Sir Launcelot setting out on a quest. They were beginning the adventure by going on a ship. And then he'd see his other sisters again, and his new nephew . . . A small flame of excitement flickered in Gavin.

Maybe Sir Launcelot had to leave people he loved too. Maybe he'd even had a dog. He had to hurt them. But that didn't keep him from his quest.

"Feel better?" said Grandad.

Gavin nodded. "A little. I'm still afraid, though." He sighed. "I'm such a coward, aren't I, Grandad . . ."

"A coward!" Grandad's moustache quivered. "You listen to me, young man — you're the bravest boy I've ever known! Everyone's afraid. Being brave is going ahead *despite* your fear. It seems to me you've done that all along. Just look at all the difficulties you've faced in this war! You're *not* a coward!"

"Really?" grinned Gavin.

"Really!" Grandad took Gavin's hand. "Let's go back into the den. You can't leave those two alone on your last night."

The train was waiting. Aunt Florence, Aunt Mary, Hanny and Norah were all crying.

Gavin had hugged Bosley for the last time as they were leaving the house. The spaniel would travel up north with the Ogilvies tomorrow, and at the end of the summer he'd go back to Montreal with Uncle Reg. Gavin could still feel the warm, wet touch of his dog's tongue on his face.

A short distance away from them Dulcie and Lucy and the Milnes were also saying tearful good-byes. "All aboard!" a man's voice called.

Norah kissed Aunt Florence last. "I will miss you *so* much!" cried Aunt Florence, releasing Norah from a bear hug.

"Thank you for *everything*!" cried Norah, laughing and crying at the same time.

Grandad kissed Aunt Mary's cheek.

"Thank you for lending us your children," she sobbed.

The old man turned to Aunt Florence, hesitated, then firmly kissed her cheek as well. Aunt Florence looked startled, then she gave him a rueful smile. "Thank you from me as well, Mr Loggin," she said quietly.

Gavin was passed from Hanny to Aunt Mary. Then he stood in front of Aunt Florence. "Goodbye," he whispered.

"Oh, my dear, *dear* little boy . . ." She pulled him

into a deep, soft embrace and he inhaled the smell of her perfume. She clung to his arms as she held him out and said gruffly, "Be brave and happy, Gavin. We'll see you next summer." Then she let him go.

"Come on, Gavin." Norah took his hand and led him onto the train, just as she had done five years earlier. They found their seats. Grandad lifted their luggage onto the rack as Norah and Gavin leaned out the window, calling and waving to their Canadian family.

"Goodbye! Goodbye!"

"Goodbye! See you next summer!"

Then the train moved out of the station and they began the long journey back to England.

Epilogue

September 28, 1945

Dear Aunt Florence, Aunt Mary and Hanny,

Thank you for your last letters. I'm glad Bosley is still okay. Uncle Reg sent me a picture of him. He looks fat! I hope Uncle Reg isn't feeding him too much.

Our house's walls are almost fixed. Grandad and his friends work on it every day. We're going to give the house a new name — Gairloch! When you come next summer it will be finished. And as soon as we move in I'm getting a dog! I've already picked it out — he's part pointer and part retriever. I've named him Kilroy.

Everyone in England rides bikes, even the

grown-ups. I am using Norah's old one. It's heavy and black and not nearly as nice as my Canadian bike.

School isn't too bad. There's only six other kids who are ten and only thirty-three in the whole school. We are the oldest age. My teacher's name is Mr Maybourne. He's also the headmaster — that's what they call "principal." He's quite strict and he complains because I'm behind the others. Some of the kids tease me about my accent and call me "Yank." I told them they should call me "Canuck" instead. Joey said I was a coward because I left England during the war. But another boy called James stuck up for me. Yesterday James came for tea. He likes all my models. You can't buy models in England any more.

Norah goes to school in Ashford. She takes the train. Next year I'll go there too, to a much bigger school where there are only boys. I'll have to wear a uniform like Norah does.

My sisters and Barry are fine. They talk about our parents all the time. Muriel says to tell you she will write soon.

The baby is funny. His hair sticks straight up. I'm trying to teach him to say "Gavin" but he won't.

Andrew came to see us! He looks just the same. He is safe and didn't get any wounds. He gave me a German badge. I'm the only person in the school who has one.

Norah has a boy friend! His name is John. He's sixteen and he goes to school in Ashford too. She met him on the train. Norah and John say they are pacifists and that the Allies shouldn't have dropped the atomic bomb on Japan. I haven't decided about that yet.

Andrew told us he's going to marry a Dutch girl called Alida. She has gone ahead to Canada to stay with his parents. They're going to live in Saskatchewan while he takes acting. I guess you know that.

Andrew and Norah and John and I went to London on the train. We saw Westminster Abbey and Big Ben. We looked for the King at Buckingham Palace but he didn't come out. Lots and lots of the buildings in London were smashed in the war, just like our house. Andrew took us to a fancy restaurant. He let me have three desserts. Then we said goodbye to him and came back all by ourselves on the train.

Gavin put down his pen and read over what he'd written. There was so much he'd left out. How the puppy he'd picked seemed afraid of him. How small and drab England was. How crowded they all were in Muriel and Barry's tiny house. The meagre food. The bitter coldness inside, now that fall — *autumn,* he corrected himself — was here. Most of all, his constant, burning homesickness.

He looked around the kitchen. Muriel was stirring a vile-smelling stew. Drying diapers were draped in front of the fire. Grandad sat in a corner behind his newspaper, puffing on his pipe. Norah was trying to concentrate on her homework at the other end of the table from Gavin.

The baby toddled over to Gavin and grabbed his leg. "Ga — win," he said clearly.

"Did you hear that?" cried Gavin. "Richard said my name!" Everyone looked up and smiled at Richard and Gavin.

Gavin picked up his pen again.

> I miss you very much and I miss Canada. I am being brave.

Thank you to Jean Little, Kay and Sandy Pearson, Patricia Runcie, Linda Shineton, Elizabeth Symon, Joan Weir — and especially to Claire Mackay for her generous advice.